MW01703015

George Christie

George Christie served as a Marine reservist and, after completing his service, became an electrician and communications troubleshooter for the Department of Defense. He prospected for the Hells Angels Motorcycle Club in 1975, becoming a full-patch member in 1976, eventually founding the Ventura, Ca charter. After which served as its President for more than thirty years international spokesman for more than twenty years. He lives in Ojai, California

MARKED

A STORY OF LIES, LOYALTY, BETRAYAL & BROTHERHOOD

DTLA Publishing LLC

a Division of DTLA Entertainment Group, LLC

MARKED

A STORY OF LIES, LOYALTY, BETRAYAL & BROTHERHOOD

A Novel by George Christie

www.georgechristie.com

 Published in the United States by DTLA Publishing, LLC, a division of DTLA Entertainment Group, LLC.

Cover designed by Joshua Hedlund / joshuahedlunddesign.com

Book designed by Christopher Johnson

ISBN-10 0-9990776-0-0 / ISBN-13 978-0-9990776-0-3

DTLA Publishing, LLC

www.dtlaent.com

Printed in the United States of America, May 2017

"To what is and what could have been, sometimes truth makes the best fiction."

Dedicated to Dick Woods
Question Mark leader & Mentor to Many

CHAPTER ONE

Sometime in the 1970's.

Early summer in the high desert of the Southwest.

0530.

Several hours had passed, and he had used the night landscape to occupy his time. The layers of the sun began revealing themselves as each second passed. It was one of the most beautiful sunrises he had seen in this lifetime, maybe in any lifetime.

The beauty of the desert is an experience that can change a man. The red hues of the rocks and cliffs, sculpted over millions of years. The big barrel cacti take the outline of bodies as the heat waves ripple upwards off their twisted forms.

The elements were starting to affect his body. The coolness of the evening was slipping away, replaced with that unforgiving oven that would bake for the next sixteen hours.

Thoughts swirled in his head. Jack knew a flash flood could change the landscape in one afternoon. What power nature had over Earth and man. But he also knew what power he held. He'd learned that fact after dispatching his first target as a U.S.

Marine scout sniper. When this afternoon was over, he would have demonstrated it once again.

Jack was lucky; the layout allowed him to position himself on top of this old barn so that the glass in the scope would not reflect off the rising sun. The rifle itself was good, but not outstanding. Nothing like a military sniper rifle you can draw from an armory.

In this type of operation, you don't get that familiar with the gear. That's because it wasn't really an operation, it was a murder. You get your tools where you can and, if you're smart, once they're used, you get rid of them. As quickly as you can, and you do it yourself.

Jack took satisfaction in the fact that he had built the silencer himself. It was crafted out of tubing, washers, and steel wool, with a threaded spacer on one end to secure it to the barrel. He hung onto that thought and contemplated whether he had become a sociopath—proud that he had created this tool to aid him in destroying another human being.

His mind drifted to his parents, may they rest in peace. How they had insisted on his getting a higher level of education. If they hadn't made such a fuss, there was a good chance he wouldn't even know what a sociopath was.

But Jack pushed these ideas out of his head as fast as they entered. He knew the heat could put strange thoughts in a man's mind, and that gave him some comfort.

CHAPTER TWO

0535.

As the sun rose, the inhabitants of the sprawling ranch house three hundred yards to the north started to stir.

Back in the late forties, the place had been owned by a local couple, Nolan and Helen Walker. This little dot in the massive 20,105 square mile nothingness of San Bernardino County may have been just more of California's unsettled frontier, but it was their home. It was the fulfillment of a dream, with plentiful underground water, horses, cattle, crops, and everything a family would need to be self-sufficient. Their dream lasted for over two decades. Then the gas companies got in touch with the Walkers, bidding for drilling rights.

Helen was against it from the beginning. "Why, after all these years of being on our own, why would we partner up?" she asked her husband. "That's not your nature. Not our nature."

"Well, Helen, if we don't," replied Nolan, "someone else will."

"Let them," argued Helen. "We got all we need."

"A family could always use a little more," was Nolan's answer.

So the corporate persuasion got to the Walkers and convinced them to lease their land for drilling. Nolan assured Helen there was nothing to worry about. This was natural gas they were after. And the company had promised him throughout their negotiations that it was completely safe.

That turned out to be a lie. The water supply became contaminated.

And Nolan and Helen's dream ended.

It had become a nightmare by the end of 1965. Both were dead from cancer. Helen went first, and then Nolan, some sixteen agonizing months later. Although his children had pleaded with him, again and again, to leave the ranch for health reasons, he stayed. It was a type of self-punishment, retribution because he felt responsible for his wife's death.

The inevitable lawsuit brought by the Walker descendants against the gas company was settled out of court. But, of course, a nondisclosure clause ensured that justice was never truly accomplished.

The Walker ranch then became part of the Walker Family Trust. It was no accident that Clarence Wade, the attorney for the trust, had also been the attorney who approached the Walkers about the drilling in the first place. They had trusted him, as everyone else in the area did.

Why wouldn't they?

Before opening his private law practice, Wade had been the County Prosecutor. He even made a run for the bench.

But Wade didn't have the knowledge or integrity to unseat the honorable and venerable Judge Orville Clark, an old-school gentleman who not only looked like Will Rogers but thought like him. A World War II hero, Clark had lost an arm and a leg in his service to his country. It hadn't made him bitter; it made him more in tune with people's everyday needs.

Clarence Wade still acted as a special prosecutor from time to time, not to serve the community, but to keep his hands in both worlds. He held the county record for conflicts of interest.

If only he had put all that energy into his family.

His oldest daughter wound up a drug addict who lost her high moral ground at an early age. She saw through her father early on and, in her heart, blamed him for her mother's alcoholism.

But all the problems in his family taught Clarence nothing. He never gave leasing out the contaminated land a second thought. He would have leased it to anybody. But he did feel it was poetic justice that the land would now hold a clubhouse for the Orphans, the second largest one-percent bike club in the world. He was sure that they had lost their souls to Satan years ago.

The Orphans were known as the Avis of the outlaw bike culture; they knew they were second best and tried harder. Their leader "Big Jim"—also known as "Jimbo"—was not a handsome man. But what he lacked in looks he made up for in money and power. And he never hesitated to wield either. Jimbo had always been big for his age, and what he had first thought of as a handicap was now a gift. His long, dirty, sandy colored hair and harsh features are taken away from his soft 6' 5" frame. When Clarence met Jimbo for the first time, all Clarence saw were dollar signs. Big Jim saw power— deal with the Devil if ever there was one.

"I'm Big Jim. I called you about the Walker place."

"Yes, yes you did," said the lawyer, shaking the big man's hand. "Pleased to meet you. You're lucky you called when you did. I've got lots of interest in that property."

"Yeah? From who?" replied Big Jim, clearly not taken in by Clarence's game. "Investigative reporters? I hear you got a health problem out there."

With the smile that had won juries over, again and again, Clarence told him, "We can fix that. It's simple. A simple fix."

"Truth be told," said Jim, looking directly into Wade's eyes, "you can't rent that place, can you, Clarence?"

Clarence held Jimbo's gaze and made a decision.

"Let's cut to the chase, Big Jim. We both know you're going to have trouble finding a place. I'm doing you a favor, here—the Orphans have a terrible reputation."

"Yeah," said Big Jim, "Well, so do lawyers. That's why I think we can accommodate each other."

As the parties sized each other up, they could each see the potential. Both these men knew that someone who could walk in both worlds built longevity in any criminal organization.

Clarence made the perfect bridge.

It didn't take them long to reach an agreement that suited both their needs. A cash deal on a handshake, no paperwork, no actual records of any kind. They could both tell any story they wanted. And they both did.

Jimbo liked that no one knew just exactly what the issue was with the Walker place, and he made sure stories abounded. The unknown would discourage people from snooping around, and that suited him just fine.

Over the next ten years or so, Big Jim and Wade made a lot of money together, the cash a perfect glue to bind their relationship.

To keep the river of money flowing, Wade built the Orphans a standing water tank on the property and supplied it with clean water brought in by truck. The tank served two functions: it fed water to the main house, which was now a safe house and clandestine headquarters, and it sent water to the barn, three hundred yards to the south. The barn was where Jimbo set up one of his early hydroponic grows. The idea was born out of a mandatory high school book report he'd been forced to complete. Sylva Sylvarum by Sir Francis Bacon may have been a bit tedious at times, but it had been very informative. Bacon's book first described the green herbal art back in 1627.

Armed with his book report, several agriculture classes, and lessons gleaned from a few failed crops, Big Jim mastered the art of the grow. There was a lot of money in dope, and Jimbo liked money more than anything.

CHAPTER THREE

0545.

Jack was watching every bit of the "stirring" through his scope. Figures were now walking in and out of the main house.

The sun had risen, but the long desert shadows were preventing Jack's eyes from adjusting. Directly in front of the house, it was still too dark to get a positive ID on his target, and Jack would take no chance on a miss. That wasn't an option. Jimbo would not give him a second shot—at least not at this location.

Jack had his thoughts and the sunrise and his weapon to support him as he waited. But he also had something else. Someone else.

Jack started nudging Robert, a little at a time, so he wouldn't startle him.

Robert spoke softly as he opened his eyes. "Okay, okay, did you see him?"

"I think everyone but him."

"It's getting light and hot," Robert said. "What are we going to do now?"

Wait…

Laying on that barn roof with Robert made Jack think of Keith, his old spotter from the Marines. Not only was Keith Jack's spotter, but he was also a true friend. Robert and Jack had also gotten close over the last few years.

Wait…

Jacks words hung in the air, settling in his chest. Had he not learned anything in this life he had lived? He wondered. As a sniper, it had never been personal. It couldn't be. Just a small image in a circle, a mist of fog escaping his target, and it was over and on to the next mission. Jack quit counting his kills not long after he started. He even convinced himself he had a special gift—a gift of no conscience.

But that whole image, the one Jack had created to keep himself sane, had come apart in a matter of seconds during his last tour in Vietnam in the jungle summer of 1968.

Jack and Keith had embarked on a clandestine mission to eliminate a VC collaborator. The mission had gone well, and they had disposed of their target. Heading back to base, they had decided to stop at a whorehouse. In Vietnam, this could just be a place where you got to know the locals. You could get a bath, a few drinks, and some fun, and then be on your way.

Under normal circumstances, the VC would not enter places occupied by U.S. military. Still, Jack and Keith both knew they were reckless.

Keith even asked Jack, "What if Charlie's there?"

Jack barked back, "Fuck Charlie!"

They both laughed, not from humor but as a release of tension. Whether from fatigue or from the arrogance of a successful kill mission, they put themselves on a collision course with destiny.

As they proceeded down the alley, Jack was overcome by a feeling that would become familiar to him as the years passed. A feeling that would serve him well.

Both Jack and Keith had their rifles slung across their backs, with their gear. As they approached the entrance to the whorehouse, a warning ran through Jack's body. He quickly unbuttoned his sidearm holster and placed his right hand on top of his .45.

As the pair crossed the threshold, they encountered four young Vietnamese men drinking around a table. The Hombres' hit song "Let it All Hang Out" played loudly on the radio. The entire scene felt surreal—as though time were suspended. The man closest to Jack locked eyes with him. The man's face reflected a lifetime of contempt for these strangers occupying his land. That contempt morphed into a rage as he reached for the Russian Tokarev TT33 pistol lying next to his drink.

Jack instinctively jerked his own weapon in response. Before the young man had control of his pistol, Jack had put two rounds in his chest. From there, he continued counter-clockwise around the table, shooting all the remaining men. The report of the shots echoed in the small room, now filled with smoke and screaming voices.

Things happened fast. As adrenaline gushed into Jack's veins, Keith appeared and delivered a shot to the head of each fallen enemy. Off to his right, another figure ran through the door towards Keith, and Jack didn't waste a second putting two rounds into the person's chest.

It took him even less time to realize what he had done.

That figure was a woman he had gotten to know—and like—over the last few months.

Jack stood frozen. Keith grabbed him, and they made their way back into the clear night air, where they could once again breathe and think.

"Fuck, fuck! What are we going to do?" said Jack. He could still hear organ music in the background as the song on the radio came to a close.

Keith came from a long line of peace officers. He understood the art of investigation. After a beat, he calmly said to Jack, "This never happened." He followed up with, "Neither one of us will ever speak of this again." He eyed Jack.

"Agreed?"

Jack nodded.

"Say it, Jack," Keith prodded, his voice still low and controlled.

Jack did, and neither man ever mentioned the incident again.

They made their way back to the jungle to delay their return to base, and when they arrived, they heard the quickly spreading story about the shootout in the whorehouse. But neither commented. They just listened.

One might think that an event like this would bring the two men closer, but it didn't. They slowly began their journeys in different directions. By the time their tour was up, they had both had enough and were ready to get back to their respective hometowns and their own versions of the American Dream.

Keith went back to Cody, Wyoming and, as expected by family tradition, became a third-generation peace officer. He joined the local Marine reserve infantry unit and took advantage of some of the best hunting and fishing in the country. It was a perfect fit. Keith adapted well to civilian life, and the violent memories he carried became distant thoughts as time passed.

But for Jack, it was a far different story.

CHAPTER FOUR

In the spring of 1969, Jack had returned to where he was born, the sleepy beach town of Ventura, California. But he really had nothing to come home to. Both of his parents were dead.

One of the things that pulled Jack back were his memories of his father taking him and his mom surf-fishing just up the coast. It had become a tradition.

Truthfully, it wasn't about the fishing. It was about the three of them spending time together. Jack's father was a defense contractor, and his mother was a homemaker, both of which afforded them weekends and long summer days for catching surf perch and the occasional shark.

But all of the togetherness was destroyed one foggy June morning during Jack's first tour in Vietnam. His parents were crossing over some railroad tracks, and something had failed with the warning lights. Their car was struck.

Jack was told his parents never knew what hit them—as if this would somehow console him. Only someone who had never suffered such a tremendous loss could actually believe that those words eased his pain.

Jack deployed again, not wanting to face the soul-deep emptiness and pain. It seemed easier to leave the family lawyer with his power of attorney, and let him settle with all the defendants named in the suit. Why would Jack want to sit around and watch everyone blame everyone else when the end result could never be changed? About ten months into his second tour, Jack got word that a settlement had been reached and that his money was being held in a trust for him.

Jack came back to an empty house to try and fill his empty heart. But sadly, all the memories of his parents raising him, with all the love and understanding a child could ask for, were no longer a part of it.

Night after sleepless night Jack surveyed each room, trying to conjure those warm feelings. He knew the drinking was just clouding his thoughts. Though he found a few things that had special meaning to him, after a couple of weeks, he came to the painful realization that his childhood home was now just a house. And he couldn't stand to be there anymore, he knew what he had to do. Jack grabbed some clothes and then entered the garage through the kitchen entrance.

And there it was, right where he had left it, carefully packed and marked in boxes: his 1942 80-inch flathead Harley. He carried the boxes, the frame, and the front end of his pickup and stacked them in the open truck bed. He piled his clothes in the cab and went back into the kitchen to see if there was anything to say goodbye to. There wasn't.

Jack took his well-weathered knife, a gift from his father, from his front jeans pocket and punctured the gas line leading to the stove. He heard the whistling of the gas as it escaped the line. He opened a book of matches and lit a cigarette. He laid the cigarette on the kitchen table, against the remaining match heads, and closed the matchbook cover.

From his truck, Jack took one last long look at his childhood home and wondered at the way things had changed. He said his final farewell, knowing that he would have to carry his memories with him.

It took quite a while for that cigarette to burn down to the match heads. Jack was almost to Old Man John's place in Somis when he caught sight of the flames. Although he wasn't sure why the sight of the flames made Jack the happiest, he'd felt in years.

Old Man John was older than Jack's dad would have been, but he felt like more of a brother to Jack than a father. Maybe it was because John was also a Marine combat veteran, from World War II. He had his own nightmares buried deep.

It had long been rumored that the old man had committed something that, by today's standards, would be considered a war crime. After a heavy day of losses on one of those godforsaken Pacific islands, a dozen Japanese soldiers had been captured.

John was left in charge of holding them until intelligence could interrogate them. But John was known to suffer an explosive temper and apparently something just snapped.

Just before sunset, John took out his Thompson machine gun, inserted a hundred-round drum, and sprayed those soldiers until all that could be heard was the clicking of his smoking weapon. John claimed that he was overrun and had no choice. It didn't matter who questioned him—that was his story, and he had stuck to it.

Lots of rumors about the old man made their way around town, but that's the one Jack hung his hat on. And after torching his parents' home, Jack's thoughts kept returning to the night in that whorehouse. He realized he wanted to talk about it. He needed someone who would not judge him, pity him, or grant him absolution, just someone who would listen.

There was, however, that matter of the commitment Jack had made to Keith; he wanted to keep his word.

After a few weeks on John's couch, and a bout of heavy drinking, the night at the whorehouse rose in Jack's throat like vomit. He knew he had a choice to make: forever swallow it or let it spew out.

"Hey, John, you see much combat?"

John started at Jack's question. "What's on your mind, Jack?"

Keeping his head down, Jack muttered, "Just making small talk."

John eyed him sharply. "No, you're not. You're fixing to tell me something. Listen, Jack, talking about it won't change a damn thing. What's done is done and can't be changed. Right or wrong, it's history."

Jack fell silent. "I just thought that it would be a way—"

John had interrupted Jack before he finished the thought. "I will tell you this: time has a way of taking the edges off hard angles. Just let it drift. We all have our demons."

John was silent for a minute, and he appeared to be on the verge of letting his own guilt and anger spill out. He changed the subject fast.

The old man was the caretaker for a movie car rental business. The business was owned by Mr. Hayward, a successful farmer. Hayward had liked the limelight of show biz and started the fledgling vehicle-and-props leasing enterprise.

John's job was to keep the vehicles serviced and running, and to fix anything that got banged up during filming. He had access to a complete machine and paint shop and, in his off hours, he had free rein to work with his real love—motorcycles.

After working on all those cars, the old man had become a bit of a movie fan himself. Not as a movie star groupie, but as an expert on writers, directors, producers, and studios. He knew what each one was looking for and learned what vehicles to present to them.

"I know you don't need the money, boy billionaire," John told Jack, "but I could use some help getting cars ready for an upcoming John Dillinger movie. I've got this guy coming over this week to check them out. His name's John Milius." The old man laughed. "You know, you might want to meet this guy; he just wrote a movie about Vietnam. He might listen to you spill your guts."

They both laughed as Jack told John to go fuck himself. Not too many people could say that to John, and Jack knew it. And he knew John was letting it go for both their sakes.

They partied into the next day.

CHAPTER FIVE

When Jack had left for boot camp in '66, Old Man John had been the head of a motorcycle club known as the Question Marks, which had been around since the mid-1950s. In the beginning, if you made it into the Marks, the old man would hand-draw the club's "center patch" with a thick black marker —a large question mark in very artistic style—onto the back of a military foul-weather jacket, worn by all the club members.

The Question Marks were one of a dozen clubs that made up the one-percenters, that one percent that the American Motorcyclist Association said was ruining the sport. The thing the AMA didn't get was that for the club members, it wasn't a sport. To the riders that made up this new outlaw brotherhood, it was a lifestyle. That "one percent" of riders wore the title like a badge.

And in fact, "1%" cloth patches were made up and distributed among the outlaw elite. When those patches showed up, the Question Marks shifted from the club's drawn-on icon to a sewn-on patch. Most of the old-timers still wore their original foul weather coats under their new denim cutoffs with the cloth patches sewn on.

By the time Jack returned from his last tour, the Question

Marks were considered the dominant club in the United States. They had eight charters up and down the West Coast, and many more independent clubs aspired to join their ranks. Jack attributed that dominance to John. It wasn't just his leadership skills that served the club well; John was the complete package.

He was the da Vinci of the bike world. He could do it all. The old man had been offered several movie parts over the years, which he'd declined. John's reputation with customers, if you were lucky enough to get to work with him, was legendary.

He had a certain way of conducting business. Jack had once helped John with a custom paint job—flames like few had ever seen. When the customer came in, John had the job on display in the middle of the shop, tank and fenders bolted to the frame.

They had agreed on a set price before the job. That was the way John did business, on a handshake. The customer started circling the bike and then tried to tell John that he really had something else in mind. It was obvious to anyone in the shop that he was trying to barter down the price. John just smiled and to everyone's amazement, grabbed the paint gun and sprayed

"No Charge" across the tank.

John could be a major pain in the ass to his friends, too.

Jack found that out firsthand as a teenager when John taught him how to turn a wrench. The old man had him mic every roller bearing that was going into every motor, one by one. Jack complained, but deep in his heart, he loved the attention he got from John.

However, Jack's close relationship with John created deep roots of jealousy in many people—both inside and outside the biker world.

CHAPTER SIX

It had been about two weeks since Jack's house burned down, and the fire inspector had ruled it arson. That opened up a criminal investigation and captured the interest of Sergeant Mike Sherman, head of the newly formed "BET" unit: Biker Enforcement Team. It had been a long time coming, but the time had finally arrived for the first shot to be fired in a war that would have no end. Sherman was a no-nonsense career cop just shy of six feet tall. His sharp, tailored uniform made him better looking than he really was. Even out of uniform he looked the part of a cop. The BET unit was made up of officers from several state agencies, but it was based in Ventura County. Their object was to stop the growth of "outlaw motorcycle gangs" - OMGs. The officers in the unit were typically single, big, and most of all white. They had to be, given that Sergeant Sherman was about as racist as they come. The sergeant's problem with men of color hadn't surfaced until his mid teens when his basketball skills were finally put to the test during his junior year at Oxnard High School. After spending a season on the bench, he gave up the sport he thought he had always excelled in. He just couldn't compete with the black players. Hell, he couldn't even earn a varsity letter. It was his first real failure in life, and he held the whole black race responsible. That ended his interest in sports and sent him in a new direction in life, the high school police explorer program. It gave Sherman a very narrow, conservative, law-and-order, view on things. The explorer, four-week, high-stress course he that attended at the Ventura Sheriffs Academy was his first exposure to this new scourge, "the outlaw biker." That's what he hung his hat on, and he swore to himself he would not fail this time. He had found purpose in life.

But though the BET men excelled in regular police units, they were now lost in a world they didn't know and would never understand.

The unit had been born a couple years before when the good sergeant petitioned the chief about the new outlaw menace that was quietly spreading. The chief, being an elected official, started counting the votes. It didn't hurt that both the chief and the sergeant could visualize the dollar signs of federal funding—which they knew could be funneled into other units for spending. They had no intention of using this money for personal gain, but over the years they had both become guilty of bending the rules for the "greater good."

If they were ever going to get the funding they coveted, they would first need arrests and, beyond that, convictions.

Law enforcement had no idea what they were about to undertake.

If any group had ever been underestimated, it was this new American-born phenomenon. Perceived at first as stupid scooter tramps, motorcycle club members would turn out to be formidable adversaries to anyone who challenged them.

In the late 1960's, the United States Air Force Base in Oxnard,

California, was hit by federal budget cutbacks. But it was also becoming part of a Ventura County expansion project, a project ironically funded by the feds. It was government efficiency at its finest.

Regardless of the comings and goings of money, the facility was experiencing definitive changes. What had been the base stockade was now the new BET unit headquarters. Under the Air Force, the stockade had served as a self-contained military lockup, and as far as Sergeant Sherman was concerned, it would continue in that tradition. The diligent cop had spent the last ninety days personally overseeing the preparation of the facility and preparing himself for his upcoming task: the elimination of the Question Marks and all that they stood for.

The first official BET meeting would focus on Jack Crest and his involvement in the arson of the Crest family home. It was somewhat symbolic that the unit's first inquiry would target Jack because he would be the focus of many multi-agency task force investigations in the years to come. As investigative grants were received and funding rolled in, law enforcement would eventually refer to BET headquarters as "the house that Jack built."

The first official meeting started with formal introductions and a general overview of how Sherman saw things. He explained as much about the Question Marks as he could: the myths, the legends, the speculations, and a lot of personal opinions. How, in the early days, they had just been an odd group of men. One observation all law enforcement could agree upon was that the Question Marks were now misfits across the board, with no productive purpose.

Sherman pivoted his lecture to the arson. It was obviously an insurance job, he told them, and this would be their first investigation, indictment, and conviction. This trifecta became the mantra of the unit—the three golden rules of BET.

The sergeant made it clear to all involved that they would go out to the Hayward ranch as a team. He explained that while the ranch was ostensibly a base for Hayward's car and prop rental business, law enforcement saw it as the Question Marks' headquarters because Old Man John was in charge and had the run of the place.

Sherman laid out more plans. He told his unit they would go to the ranch in five unmarked cars. They were to display solidarity and show they were serious; they would all wear custom-made BET jackets. The jackets were light but durable dark-blue work jackets with "Biker Enforcement Team" emblazoned across the back, and the letters "BET" across the left breast, all embroidered with white stitched letters. Sherman didn't mention to his men, however, that he'd had them made by the same company that supplied most of the bike and car clubs with their jackets.

The entire unit approached the main workshop of the ranch. Several bikes sat out front and men were filing out of the tin building. It was an impressive sight: five new black undercover cars strategically facing the entrance. As both groups of men rallied around their leaders, John spoke first.

"What do you need, Sergeant?"

"We came to talk to Jack Crest."

"Maybe you should go by his house," John suggested, causing

the men around him to break into laughter.

Sherman glared at John.

Not one to avoid confrontation, Jack stepped forward. "What do you need, Sergeant?"

All eyes were on Sherman. It was his move, and he got right to the point. "I have a probable cause warrant for your arrest, for the arson of what was your parents' home."

Jack stared right into the sergeant's hard eyes. "Why would you think I had anything to with that?"

"For the insurance," replied Sherman. "It's obvious to us in the BET unit."

It didn't take long for Sherman to seize this golden moment, to explain what the new unit was all about and what their goal was.

"What kind of fucking crew you running here?" Jack barked back at Sherman. "Insurance fraud? There was no insurance on that house!"

The subconscious was something that had interested Jack from an early age. The reason he had chosen not to renew the home insurance was something he would contemplate for years to come. Had his subconscious known his ultimate intentions and guided his actions? Or was it just dumb luck? He supposed it didn't matter at this point.

"Looks like you need to work on your investigative technique, Sergeant," said Jack. "Now either arrest me or get the fuck out of here."

Jack wasn't sure where his outburst came from, given that he was normally quiet and reserved, but out it came. It was a tense moment that lasted a seeming eternity. Jack saw Old Man John shoot him an approving glance.

The only response from the BET officers as they departed was Sherman saying he would be seeing them all very soon.

CHAPTER SEVEN

BET wasn't the only government agency interested in Jack Crest.

"Sarge, there's two feds here," Sherman was told when he returned from the ranch. "They've been waiting for you."

"Well, who let them in?" The sergeant didn't like anyone encroaching on his domain.

"Don't know. They were here when we got back."

Sherman walked into his office. "Make yourselves at home, gentlemen," he said dryly.

One of the men made the introductions. "Bob Ingram, former Navy Intelligence. And this is Bill Bradley, formally of the National Security Council, special group, covert operations. We are now both attached to the FBI. We have a professional request."

Sherman nodded.

"We need to petition Jack Crest about his services. His military background makes him a possible covert asset," Ingram said. "So we need you to suspend any investigations involving him."

Sherman inhaled sharply. "You've got to be shittin' me."

"No," said Bradley calmly. "we're not. And it would not only be appreciated if you show us this professional courtesy, but it could also generate a lot of important relationships for your unit in the future." Bradley locked eyes with Sherman. "I suggest you discuss this with your chief, who will further explain the imperativeness of your support."

Sherman remained silent, continuing to glare at the two men.

"We all have the same goals, Sergeant," said Bradley finally. "Just different methods. Thanks for your time, and we'll be in touch."

His unwanted visitors had scarcely left his office when Sherman had the chief on the phone. His boss impressed upon him the opportunity this request could afford them, though the conversation fell short of a direct order. Although he wasn't happy about it, Sherman decided to stand down and see where this new development would lead them.

Slightly east of BET headquarters, the Question Marks were holding a special meeting of their own. Since the club's inception, its meetings had progressed from informal bull sessions, with drinking and any other vices available, to the currently structured states of decorum. That was fine with Jack. After his military service, these meetings contained just the right amount of discipline.

Before the meeting was called to order, several members pointedly expressed that they felt the visit to the ranch was a personal issue between Jack and the cops. These members were from the same clique that Jack knew took exception to his being financially independent. Rumors had run wild about just how much he was worth when the papers featured a story about an undisclosed settlement in his parents' deaths. The sentiments were usually amplified by booze and drugs.

Sensing the tension in the room, Jack asked for the floor after roll call. He knew he needed to face the issue head on. Jack stood as he addressed his brothers. This would become a standard for him when he was passionate about a subject. He first apologized for bringing all the heat on the ranch. He then asserted that he had no idea who started the fire or why and that the subject was now closed as far as he was concerned.

Next, Jack went on to explain that anyone who thought the BET unit had been set up because of a house fire was in denial as to what the future had in store for them. And, he told them, if any member was not prepared to give up his freedom or his life for what this lifestyle stood for, he should move on.

The meeting erupted into outbursts of personal opinions. John took control of the room, demanding order.

He recognized Smokey. Smokey had a long goatee that was braided into several strands, giving him the appearance of a pirate. At just short of six feet tall, with dirty Levi's, a ratty vest, and his brown hair combed back tight, he looked every bit the old-school biker. Most of the parts on Smokey's bike had been "borrowed," never to be returned, or just outright stolen. Jack knew that to Smokey, Jack was part of a new breed of bikers, one Smokey wasn't entirely comfortable with.

It had nothing to do with Jack's money—Smokey had no problem spending other people's money. It was the structure and discipline that had slowly made its way into the biker culture that created the friction. Smokey made it clear that this wasn't the fucking Marines, and that he didn't like the direction the club was heading.

In the beginning, the Question Marks had simply had a leader, and everyone followed him until he could no longer lead. Now their leader had the title of "President," and they were filling up all the obvious offices that any other club would elect. As Smokey addressed the room, he told them he had just about had his fill of all the new rules and regulations that were being shoved down their throats. He went on to say he was not impressed with the BET unit, and that as far as he was concerned, things were changing too fast. Maybe no one else was ready to speak up, but he was tired of keeping quiet.

John addressed the room next, countering that they had all accepted the responsibility that was overtaking them when they made the decision to expand their club. He reminded them that it had been by unanimous vote that they had opened their ranks to other areas and new charters.

Jack suggested that they should adjourn the meeting. He would have his attorney, who had a top-notch field investigator, find out as much information as he could about the new BET unit.

In closing, John reminded everyone there would be elections next week.

The meeting ended with a commentary free for all, as was customary. It was a group therapy session before anyone even knew what that was. Jack was surprised that this weekly ritual didn't elicit more physical confrontations; it cleared the air more often than not.

As the members broke into small groups, their attention shifted from club business to what had brought them all to this lifestyle initially: motorcycles.

The main topic was the annual ride to Sturgis, South Dakota. Question Mark chapters from all over would meet up at the huge Black Hills Rally to swap stories for bragging rights around the main fire in the campground. They'd be staying at the same place they'd stayed the last several years, and their presence along with the all-night parties was starting to take its toll on the attendance of other campers. John had discussed the issue with Jáck, to see if Jack could come up with a resolution to the problem—an act symbolizing John's deep trust in the Jack.

When Jack left for the Marines, he had said goodbye to John as a rowdy teenager but returned as a disciplined man. Jack sensed an immediate respect from John upon his return, and the feeling was mutual.

As proof of that respect, the old man had loaned Jack one of Hayward's movie rental bikes while his own bike was being rebuilt. The loaner was a 741 Indian Scout with a tank shift and girder front end, fire engine red with a hot-rod motor that would send any big stock twin back to the shop for a tune-up. It was a fun ride, but there was one thing wrong with it: it wasn't Jack's flathead. His bike would be ready for the run to Sturgis, but for now, the Scout served his needs.

Jack had come back from Vietnam to a different club, with different members, and he was taking his time in evaluating everyone who was part of this new commitment he had made.

He especially liked a young prospect named Robert, a lean and lanky six-foot-two Texas transplant who had grown up as a Navy brat at Point Mugu Naval Air Station. In twelve years, Robert had attended fifteen different schools. The family had followed their father wherever the Navy sent him. The new kid was always tested, and Robert had learned to answer with his fists.

The young Texan had a good look and a unique style. He wore black Frisco jeans with a leather strip on the inside of the right pant leg to protect it from his shotgun-straight pipes that could burn a hole there in no time. He wore wool shirts, tall black engineer boots, and a silver chain that connected his worn leather wallet to his belt loop. He also sported a black leather vest, while everyone else had a denim cut-off. Jack wasn't sure if Robert was the very first to make the switch, but he definitely was the one who made it look cool.

One morning, as spring turned to summer, the pack had been headed southbound on Highway 99 after a long weekend of riding and partying. To everyone's amazement, Robert removed his winter gloves and cut off the fingers.

He was always the trendsetter. He would fight with you at the drop of a hat and then insist on buying you a drink as he dusted you off. The women couldn't stay away or keep their hands off of him. He rode an outside oiler panhead in a '57 straight-leg frame with a cut-down five-gallon tank and a turned-down wide glide front end. In an era when everyone said you could not have enough chrome, Robert used it only to highlight his blacked-out machine.

He was style.

At the beginning of their initiation into a club, prospects wore a bare cut. This lets the outlaw brotherhood know they would soon be part of the one-percent nation if they could hold their mud. The unwritten rules in this esoteric culture were built on common sense and respect. Back then, if someone was wearing a sleeveless vest and not prospecting for a club, that vest would be cut off his back.

Of course, trying to enforce that tradition in the modern world would be a full-time job. But that's exactly how Robert had encountered Old Man John, at the Rock Store in Malibu Canyon. The Rock Store was a Sunday afternoon hangout, a place to show off your bike and have a beer. It wasn't a bar, just a mom-and-pop store serving to the locals. It was surrounded by huge oak trees and lots of parking. Club members were known to ride out there from time to time, not for fun, but to keep a pulse on what was new in the fast-growing society they were the center of.

On that day, Robert saw two strangers pull into the middle of the lot, acting like they belonged there. Back in the day, you could tell where someone was from by the style of the bike they rode because a rider couldn't go to the Harley dealership or an aftermarket shop, to get accessories. No one sold custom parts; you had to make them. But these guys didn't look they were from anywhere, and each one was sporting a vest.

Robert saw two club members—whom he knew to be Smokey and John—looking them over. "This could get interesting," he thought.

"You see, this is what I am talking about," he heard Smokey say to Old Man John.

John broke the silence with a simple question. "Where's the rest of your mob?"

The bigger of the two answered back. "Who wants to know?"

This was definitely going to get real ugly and quick. Robert glided nonchalantly into the fighting range of the foursome.

"You need to answer the man," pressed Smokey, starting to move in. But John extended his arm across Smokey's chest. "Hold on," he said smiling broadly, glancing ever-so-slightly at Robert.

The bigger of the two newcomers pulled back his right arm to deliver a punch. Just as he got in position to throw, Robert's right cross came from the shoulder. A shorter distance of travel gave Robert the jump on delivery, and he felt the man's jaw shift, indicating that he had knocked out the stranger.

Robert pivoted to focus on the man's companion, but he had taken off from the surrounding trees.

Robert watched in silence as John pulled the sleeveless vest off the limp body. Reflexively his hands went up to catch it as it was thrown to him.

"I think this is yours."

Robert didn't waste a beat putting on the vest. All three jumped on their bikes and rode west into the sun.

It was at that moment that Robert became hypnotized by the two large Question Mark patches bouncing along in front of him.

After the meeting, Jack invited Robert to ride over to his Uncle Pete's bar and restaurant in the middle of Oxnard, the next town over. They would have some dinner and a couple of drinks and then drift out into the night.

Robert was delighted at Jack's invitation. For a prospect to accompany a full patch holder—especially one of Jack's stature—was a true honor. As they rolled out onto the main road, Robert followed protocol and yielded the lead to Jack. Though he would never admit it out loud, he preferred that position because riding a half a bike length back gave him a great view of Jack's back. As he watched the question mark bounce around in the wind, he was confident he would soon earn his. But right now it was still a dream.

The feeling he felt that day riding behind John and Smokey was now even stronger as he gazed at the back of Jack's vest as they pulled in front of Uncle Pete's place.

CHAPTER EIGHT

Jack loved his Uncle Pete and could count on him dropping whatever he was doing when he heard the bikes. Uncle Pete would come out to greet him and anyone with him. Pete had come from the East Coast and married into Jack's family. He had always seemed a bit of a gangster. He was exotic and mysterious, and that was just fine with Jack. Pete was average height, barrel-chested, dark complexioned, with a heavy beard and half a cigar ever-present in his mouth.

Jack had worked for Pete from time to time when he was a kid, but Jack's mother and dad always frowned on it. Later in life, he found out why. Some of the patrons who frequented the bar were notorious. The most infamous, gangster Mickey Cohen, would come up a couple times a month and hold court in the farthest booth in the back. When Jack's mom found out, it was the last straw. Jack could still hear her: "There's a goddamn hit on that Jew! Our family has nothing against the Jews or anyone else for that matter. We're Greeks who run a kosher-style restaurant, but this could bring trouble!"

That ended Jack's "employment" with Uncle Pete.

Uncle Pete was the only one who could get away with calling Jack "Jackie," and now with the settlement, he even called him "moneybags" from time to time.

As Jack and Robert turned off their thundering bikes, Pete yelled at him, "Jesus Christ, Jackie! I'm trying to run a fucking business here!"

Pete extended his hand to Robert.

"Peter Bokron." He always introduced himself with his full name. "Come in and eat. Come on. Come on. We're getting ready to close soon."

When Jack or any of his friends ate at Pete's, they ate what he gave them. He'd tell them to try the short ribs and, no matter what they wanted, they got the special of the day. But that was okay. The food was always good, and no matter how much Jack insisted, his uncle would always say, "Goddammit, your money's no good here!"

Still, Jack always left enough money on the table to cover things, and he felt Pete respected that. He'd let whatever girl waited on Jack keep the money, so it all worked out.

Pete also busted Jack's balls a little. Over the years he did it right in front of whoever Jack was with.

"Goddammit, Jackie," he said, as they were finishing up their meal, "right back on that fucking motor."

Motor. That was the word that he—and most of his generation—used when they referred to a bike.

"You should have stayed in the corps," he said, continuing his rant. "The base commander himself told me they really wanted you to stay in, Jackie." He was referring to the brass at the Port Hueneme Seabee base. Uncle Pete knew everybody in Ventura County, and he enjoyed letting everyone know that he did.

"How would he know, Pete?" Jack said. "He's Navy."

"The Marines are part of the Navy, buddy boy!"

With Pete's response, Jack felt his intuitions getting the better of him, just like the night of the shootout in that whorehouse. Jack knew this was a gift he needed to cultivate.

There was more to this, but neither one pushed the subject. They said their goodbyes and then rode off into the night.

It was late by the time Jack and Robert made it back to the ranch. They came in a back way, on Highway 118, with their bikes wide open.

Any meeting night, you could count on members milling around until the sun came up the next morning. The small group left around the fire could hear the straight pipes on Jack and Robert's bikes echoing in the distance. With each crackle of the fire, the pipes bellowed louder and louder until the fire was a silent bright light and all they could hear was the retort of the pipes. Modified to amplify.

Robert jumped into what was left of the party, but Jack called it a night. He unrolled his bedding in the bed of his truck and lay down to wait for the morning sun to reveal itself.

When Jack awoke a few hours later, the party was over. That was okay with him; he needed some time to himself. His stomach was as empty as his surroundings, so he jumped on the Scout and went to the local food joint, the Frontier Café, where he was a regular. He sat at his usual table in the back, facing the door—he couldn't let anyone get the jump on him.

Emma, the old waitress who worked the breakfast shift, greeted him as she set up his table.

"Let me guess. A stack of pancakes, side of sausage, and a black coffee?"

Jack joked with her about how she could read his mind and asked her what he was thinking now.

"You have a dirty mind for a young man!" she shot back at him.

They both had a good laugh. After a couple sips of coffee, he slipped into the bathroom.

When Jack returned, what he found at his table didn't sit well with him. The same two feds who had been waiting at BET headquarters for Sherman were now waiting for him.

"Two more coffees?" Emma yelled to Jack across the dining area.

"Sure, and I could use a warm-up."

The three men sat in silence, sipping their coffees as they measured each other up.

Bob Ingram spoke first, introducing himself as he had to Sherman: "Navy Intelligence."

Ingram was a small man in his late thirties. Jack noticed an Annapolis class ring on his slight, smooth hands. Just one look at those hands told Jack that this was not a field agent; the man was an analyst.

Something was off, and Jack knew he couldn't trust him. He didn't like the way Ingram continually blinked his eyes and diverted his attention around the room. His wrinkled suit didn't fit quite right, and his shoes were a dull black. Jack considered giving him the benefit of the doubt on that front. Maybe Ingram had been on the road the last few days, contributing to his less-than-stellar appearance.

Sitting to Ingram's right was the second half of the fed duo, Bill Bradley, introduced as part of the National Security Council's "special" covert operations group.

Bradley's presence caught Jack's attention. He was a compact fighting package with short-cropped hair and piercing gray eyes. His face carried a scar that ran from above his left eye down to his jaw line, which he wore like a medal. His ethnicity could change with his dress; he was the perfect operative.

It was soon obvious that what the early-fortyish Bradley lacked in formal education, he made up for in hands-on experience. Jack suspected that Bradley had started on the ground floor as a Navy Seal and then made the transition to covert activities. Jack recognized Bradley as a killer who would in all likelihood kill again.

Jack had heard about how potential operatives are probed by covert ops, and he realized what was taking place. Jack's service file contained things of obvious interest to them, but also certain subtleties, like his ability to keep his mouth shut, which he had proven in several situations. One, in particular, had caught their eye.

During an advanced combat training operation at Camp

Pendleton Jack had been on a scouting patrol with his platoon leader. Returning to base camp, they found the two Marines at the forward listening post sound asleep. The sergeant put his index finger to his lips and spoke in a low voice.

This is how Marines get killed.

Jack said nothing as the sergeant pulled the pin on an illumination grenade that he nonchalantly tossed in the foxhole. The platoon leader pulled Jack into the bush, and they watched in silence as the two sleeping Marines came to life. What the sergeant intended to be a valuable learning experience turned into a base controversy. The two Marines, in fear and confusion, not only abandoned their post but left their weapons and gear behind. They also both suffered burns and temporary blindness. Mishaps like this happen all the time in the field, but this time one of the sleeping Marines was the nephew of a United States congressman, and the politician wanted answers. It was Jack that put the story together that saved the sergeant from a court marshal. No matter how hard the provost marshal pushed on Jack, he explained that when they approached the post, it appeared empty. After they had given the password several times with no response, they were confident the Marines in the listening post had retreated closer to the base camp, as planned. The last exercise of the evening would be the use of an illumination device, and if the Marines had not fallen asleep on watch, there would have been no incident or injuries.

It was obvious to everyone that this was not how the incident occurred, but Jack was steadfast in his position that it was an accident. This was just fine with the company chain of command, and Jack was rewarded for being a good Marine. He came out of the training a PFC.

Ingram opened his soft brown leather briefcase and pulled out a file that read JACK CREST in bold black letters on the cover. Over the name was stamped the word CLASSIFIED. Jack's ego came into play, and that's what these two men were banking on.

They started with a few questions about some classified operations. Jack sat in silence and listened. They moved on to some questions about the use of narcotics taking place in the military but explained they were just looking for background information. There would be no charges brought against anyone.

They made it clear Jack was not the target but wanted to know if the distributors were also users. Jack stopped them.

"You didn't come all this way to ask me questions you already know the answers to," Jack said. "What's really on your minds?"

Ingram spoke first. "The government has a lot of money and time invested in you, and we would like to know if you're prepared to give anything back."

"I thought that's what I had done the last few years."

"That was a good start," shot back Bradley, "but only a down payment. The world is changing, and we are asking you—your country is asking you—to make that transition with us. Your lifestyle is the perfect cover. You can move in circles that would put others at great risk. Your life would basically be as it is now, except that from time to time, you would be called upon to serve your country."

Jack again fell silent, staring at the two men that he knew were playing him.

He could feel his temper getting the better of him—a weakness that had plagued him since childhood. It always started with a smile, and then erupted into anger. All his discipline as a Marine Scout Sniper was powerless against it; this was up close and personal.

When Jack spoke, he addressed both men, but he kept his eyes on Bradley, who had been doing most of the talking. "I've done my last mission for my country."

"You really think so?" said Bradley.

"Yes, I do," Jack replied.

"So you work for yourself now?"

"I don't work for anybody."

Bradley smirked. "Don't fool yourself, Jack. We all serve a master in one form or another."

Trying to control his boiling anger, Jack shot back, "Maybe, but you two are nothing more than errand boys."

Bradley's smirk became a flat line. "Perhaps. But the bigger the errand, the larger the payoff."

Jack shook his head. "I have all I need."

"Yes, so I hear." Bradley reached into his left breast pocket and pulled out a silver cigarette case. "Want a smoke? They're imported. Oh, and I want you to know that this is the last thing I'll offer you."

He pushed the release, exposing a row of unfiltered cigarettes. He extended the case to Jack in a last symbolic gesture.

Jack was not against helping his country, but not like this. Not with these feds.

Jack stared Bradley straight in the eye. "Fuck you!"

The stare down was interrupted by Ingram stating the obvious. "It looks like we're done here." With that, the two men got up and left, leaving Jack to his cold breakfast.

Unbeknownst to Jack, the two men had one more stop to make before they made their flight at the naval air station. Bradley waited in the car as Ingram entered BET headquarters. One of the young BET members greeted Ingram and told him the sergeant was waiting for him in his office. Ingram opened his briefcase and threw a copy of Jack's file on Sherman's desk.

"This file is for your eyes only," he instructed Sherman. "We want you to put pressure on Crest and his associates, and this file will assist you. Jack's associates are fair game, but no indictments on Crest without clearance from me. I'm sure your chief explained how important your cooperation is."

They shook hands and Ingram made his way back to Bradley and his transportation home.

As the sergeant read Jack's file, jealousy rose up from his stomach into his throat. Sherman had never done military duty, and this was always a self-imposed shortcoming in his mind.

He had already decided to go along with the request from Ingram, the strange little man from Washington D.C. But Sherman had his own motives for cooperating with Ingram and Bradley. He had no pretense that he was doing this for any of the "right" reasons—if there even were any to be found. He was intent on what he could personally glean from this arrangement. Sherman planned on becoming Ingram and Bradley's right-hand man.

He wouldn't find out until much later that was the hand they wiped their asses with.

CHAPTER NINE

Jack remained in the restaurant, thinking about the unexpected meeting he'd just had. Emma cleared the plates and gave him one last shot of coffee as he readied himself to leave. He needed time to sort things out in his mind. Or better yet, push it out of his head altogether.

He decided on the latter. He jumped on the Scout and pounded through the gears on the tank shifter. In no time, he found himself on the coast highway at the spot where he grew up surf fishing with his parents. The familiar surroundings were comforting and provided refuge for him whenever he needed to think.

Jack shifted his thoughts to the unfinished club business he needed to clear up. There was an issue with some of the original members, one that had arisen in his absence. That was the politics of the club. If you weren't around, you were in danger of becoming the focus of a witch-hunt, whether real or imagined.

Jack's current problem had been brought about by another old-school member, Dave, who just returned from a three-year stretch in San Quentin behind a marijuana distribution conviction. Dave was a stocky Mexican-American who didn't like blacks or Latinos, especially if they happened to be from Texas. His intolerance started the day he arrived at the prison, and it stemmed from the treatment he received from several black guards. But the hatred toward his own race started and ended with Corrections Officer Victor Lopez from Houston, Texas. A short, fat man, Lopez watched Dave's every move and reported every action with constant infraction reports that deprived Dave of his simple privileges. It became a war of wills that Dave took out on anyone in the prison population he suspected of collaborating with prison staff. He walked the prison yard daily and stuffed the Question Mark name down the throats of anyone foolish enough to cross him.

It wasn't that he was a skilled fighter. He wasn't. What gave him an edge was that he would let his opponent beat on him until they were exhausted, all the while telling them it would soon be his turn to dish out the pain. The exhaustion amplified by the consuming fear soon took its toll on his victims. Some of them pleaded, some cried, but whether it was with pain or fear, they all paid the price.

Dave was as fierce as they came, and his bid in prison had not helped his disposition. If ever there was an argument against the existing penal experiment, Dave was living proof. With no regard for society, they opened the prison doors one foggy afternoon and unleashed this once-introverted man back into the world.

Dave now refused to sit in a room with a closed door—and this included the front door. And he felt that anyone in the outlaw world who wasn't an original Question Mark owed him something and was fair game.

In Dave's eyes, Jack was not from the original crew. The fact that Jack had been wearing one of John's hand-drawn Question Marks jackets prior to leaving for the Marines meant nothing to Dave. As far as Dave was concerned, Jack was a kid who left by choice, and that was a problem that would always exist in Dave's convoluted thought process.

Old Man John watched this issue brewing and, rather than try to resolve it diplomatically, he pushed it into a showdown. When Dave complained to John about Jack's place in the club, John pushed back with comments that Jack wasn't a kid anymore.

In fact, he suggested Dave let it go, which John knew would never happen. John knew that at some point Jack would have to reestablish himself and he figured better now than later, and what better way than within the mother charter itself? This would give John the answer to the pressing question: Could Jack step up as a leader?

It was mid-afternoon by the time Jack got back to the ranch. John recognized the sound of the straight shotgun pipes on the red Scout and made his way through the steel roll-up door.

As soon as Jack saw John, the lines on the old man's weathered face told him there was something on his mind.

"What's up, Grandpa?" Jack barked at him, to cut the seriousness of the moment.

The two men walked out toward the man-made pond. When they reached the bank, John lit a joint, drew a long pull on it, and then extended it to Jack. They stood in silence passing it back and forth until John popped the still-burning end in his mouth and swallowed it down his throat.

John spoke first. "A lot of things have changed, my young friend. Sometimes I wish I could go back in time. I'd keep things like they were in the old days."

"You know," answered Jack, "that's called hindsight, and it's not a luxury we have in this life, John. I'm happy with where we're heading, and I hope we do it together."

The old man replied, "Dave's a different guy since he got out and he thinks he has a problem with you."

"Is it a real problem," asked Jack, "or an imagined one? Because a real problem can be fixed. But imagined? That's another story."

"I really don't know, Jack."

"How 'bout I go see him tonight at his house and get this straight between us."

"I think you should. But you need to understand that Dave's really not the guy you knew anymore."

"You know something, John? Neither am I." With that, Jack made plans for the night. It would start with a quick stop for dinner at his uncle's diner, which would give him a chance to see if Pete knew anything about his two visitors from the government, and to fuel up for what could become a long night with Dave.

Over dinner, Uncle Pete didn't mention the military but told Jack that his godfather Nick wanted to see him. Nick was a tall, good-looking Greek who always had a different beautiful woman in his company. He'd introduce each of them as his fiancée; and as a kid, Jack bought into that for awhile. Nick was always late for something and never failed to tell you after a few minutes he had to be on his way.

Jack joked with Uncle Pete, "Well, tell Nick I'm sorry I missed him, but I was late for something." They both had a good laugh, and Jack rode off to the west end of Oxnard.

As he made his way through town, he thought about his conversation with John, and about how John really was becoming an old man. When he pulled in front of Dave's, he saw that the yard was littered with fifty-gallon drums lying on their sides with the tops cut off. In front of each barrel was a post driven into the ground with a short piece of heavy-duty chain connected to it. At the end of each chain was a pit bull, looking lean and mean. The chains popped like steel whips each time the dogs lunged forward. No dog could reach the other and this added to the frenzy.

Jack made his way through this maze toward Dave, who was standing on the porch. The look in his eyes was fueled by alcohol and cross-top meth tabs. His girlfriend, Darcie, was standing behind him, dressed all in skintight leather riding gear. Her perfect body made up for her less-than-perfect face. Both Dave and Darcie sported black eyes, inflicted by each other.

Rumor had it that Dave had slapped Darcie in one of their recent whiskey-fueled escapades and left her with her shiner.

The next morning, Darcie returned the favor with a right cross while Dave was driving his prized '53 Chevy. She diverted Dave's attention, so that he turned his head away from the first launched from her perfectly positioned body, and then turned his head back just in time for her fist to catch his eye.

"Take that, you motherfucker!" she'd yelled as she leaped into the backseat, out of Dave's reach. She was no fool.

As Dave pulled over to issue out his retribution, Darcie jumped out the back door before the car had even stopped, disappearing over the nearest fence.

Apparently, the loving couple had reunited. Jack wondered at the wisdom of having chosen this night to sort out his and Dave's problems. Dave was surely already feeling a fair amount of stress.

Jack continued to maneuver his way through the minefield of pit bulls while Dave's eyes followed his movements. His glare got more sinister by the second. Jack entered the house, and it was easy to tell by the empty bottles and glasses that this little soirée was at least into its second night. The longer Dave was up, the deeper into the abyss he ventured.

Although Jack didn't know her well, Darcie made it a point to give him a warm welcome home. Dave interrupted Darcie's impromptu homecoming embrace with, "Hey, Jack. Someone here wants to see you." Jack awkwardly broke Darcie's hold and crossed the threshold into the lion's den.

Sitting in an overstuffed chair was another Dave—David Brown—also one of the original Marks. He was rangy with shoulder-length dirty blond hair and a large mustache and goatee. He could have passed for Wild Bill Hickok, and the old Western-style pistol stuck in his waistband added to his cultivated image. Next to him were two crutches that helped him get around on two broken legs.

Brown had been in what was now his second accident, a grinding mess of road rash and reinjures. The steel rods that had been inserted in his two tibias from his first wreck were now both bowed to the left from this second collision. He was waiting for surgery to have new rods inserted. The mere fact that he had survived two major motorcycle accidents made him a miracle of modern medicine. His motto was "better living through chemistry," and he practiced what he preached.

As Jack entered, Brownie gave his usual greeting, "Que paso, brother? Excuse me if I don't get up." He extended his hand, which held several bottles of pills. "Up, down or sideways?" he asked, with his intoxicating smile and voice.

Jack dropped to one leg and greeted Browning with a hug, passing on the offer of drugs.

Surveying the room, Jack felt a little awkward. He knew he should be relaxed and comfortable with his brothers, but out of military habit, he continued until he was satisfied with his observations. But the only person who presented even a remote possibility of trouble was the person he had come to see.

Brownie was armed; he always was. And although he never hesitated to use his weapon when needed, he'd never use it on a club brother.

There were others in the house, too, a handful of hang-arounds and wannabes. Maybe this was some kind of happy group therapy session to help Dave and Darcie slide back into the bliss of a warm and loving relationship.

On second thought, probably not.

Darcie had run all the girls off hours ago, and maybe a couple of guys too. The ones left were arguing about the art of dog fighting—what breed was the best, where the best dogs were from and, most importantly, who had the best dogs. Dave turned to Jack and asked his opinion.

"I don't really know much about dog fighting," Jack replied, curtly.

Dave was starting to push now, and Jack knew it.

"What?" replied Dave. "You leave your opinion in the Marines?"

"No, I got an opinion."

"Oh? What's that, Jack?"

The two men stared at each other until the room became uncomfortable.

Jack's voice cut across the room. "Dog fighting is not an art."

Dave forced a couple chuckles. "Is that right?"

The remaining guests shifted uncomfortably in their chairs, not wanting to take sides.

Dave became enraged in their attempt to satisfy both his and Jack's egos.

His anger shifted from guest to guest, and the more he questioned them, and the more they spoke up, the more entangled they became in the web Dave was spinning around each potential victim.

"You're talking out of both sides of your neck!" Dave bellowed.

It was now obvious to Jack that the rumors about Dave's temper were not exaggerated. With the skill of a chess master, Dave pitted each of the pawns in the room against the other. He slowly rose out of his chair like a vampire rising from sleep.

Dave shuffled across the room to two men who had been foolish enough to voice their opinions. The pills Brownie had passed out were now affecting his motor skills. Dave stood over the bigger one of the two and pointed at the smaller one. "I think he's scared."

For a brief moment, the man Dave was standing over seemed relieved that he was not the focus of Dave's wrath. Until Dave said, "And I think you're glad he is. You two motherfuckers are going to settle this once and for all."

Both men tried feebly to neutralize the uncompromising situation. "There's nothing to settle. It's all good," they insisted.

The men looked around the room for a flicker of support, but it was not there. Dave pulled the larger man to his feet and pushed him into the other man as if he were pitting two fighting dogs at one other. They collided, and then both men broke the door—a door that was always open since Dave's return from prison. Out into the night, they ran, zigzagging through the dogs.

The remaining guests started to make their exit.

Dave shuffled around the room some more, engaged in an esoteric conversation with himself. Darcie was talking shit to Dave, calling him a bully. She knew how to push his buttons.

And timing is everything.

He told her to shut the fuck up, and if she didn't, he was going to turn her out.

"Maybe a good fucking from Jack is exactly what I need," was her answer. It wasn't what Dave wanted to hear.

She looked over at Brownie, who was now passed out, and then back at Dave. "You fucking losers are a joke," she said. Then she broke into laughter, which pushed Dave over the edge.

Dave turned his focus to Jack, and that's what this was really all about.

"So you came here to fuck Darcie!" he screamed.

Jack's own anger was starting to rise. "No, I'm here to see you."

That meant nothing. Dave had reached the point of no reason. "What! Are you too good to fuck behind a Mexican?" he asked.

"You're talking out your ass, Dave. Why don't you shut the fuck up?"

"Why don't you shut me up, big boy?" Dave replied.

It started with a stare down and then Dave shuffled his way over to Jack. He stood over Jack, breathing heavily and mumbling to himself.

Although Jack was overcome with rage, he showed no emotion. As he started to rise, Dave grabbed him by the front of his cut with both hands. This was fine with Jack. As long as Dave was holding him with both hands, he wasn't hitting.

Jack brought both his arms over the top of Dave's and applied pressure, not only to control him but to measure his strength. The pair tumbled backward onto the wooden coffee table, right onto Darcie's miniature elephant collection. The table splintered and the pair fell through to the floor.

Somehow Dave was on top, but Jack still had control of Dave's arms with the hold he had applied. Whether it was to help Jack or to get the both of them off her elephants, Darcie rolled them, and Jack was suddenly on top. Jack broke free and jumped to his feet. But Dave was right in front of him, and they squared off once again.

As they bounced off the walls, Darcie tried to stay ahead of them, holding a box with one hand, collecting what she held valuable to her with the other and placing it into the box. As she yelled insults at Dave, she also shut the doors that led to other areas of the house. Dave and Jack were now isolated in the large front room.

By the end of the scuffle, all the wooden furniture was broken or at the very least turned over. Somehow they managed not to fall into—or wake up—Brownie, who was passed out in the same chair he had been in for days.

Jack uprighted a couple chairs, and they both took a much-needed break. Dave drifted off into sleep, mumbling under his breath until it turned into a loud snore. Jack sat there until the sun entered the still-open front door. He dozed but avoided falling into any kind of serious sleep. He wanted to be alert when Dave came to.

Brownie awoke before Dave. Jack watched his eyes widen as he focused in on the room. "Jesus Christ, what the hell happened?"

"Dave had a couple things he wanted to explain to me," Jack explained calmly.

"Yeah, I think I heard something about that," Brownie said with a sly smile. Jack could hear the respect in his voice. They both knew that leaving this situation to brew is something a one-percenter just would not do.

When Dave awoke, Jack was staring right at him. "Is there anything else you want to talk about?" Jack asked.

Dave surveyed the room. Then he looked at Jack. "It looks like we covered it all last night. But if I think of anything I'll let you know."

Jack smiled back. "You do that, brother."

With that, they said their goodbyes and Jack was in the wind heading back to the ranch. He came through the back route as he often did, to see if anyone was at the café. He spotted a couple bikes out front and slammed on his rear break as he downshifted his way into the parking lot.

John looked up as Jack entered the dining room. John and Robert were stationed in the back as always, with a United States road map spread out across the table. John took a puff on his cigar, and the smoke drifted upwards while the ashes settled on top of the map. With a red felt pen, John followed the highways that would take them through at least six states to their destination: Sturgis, South Dakota. He plotted their course as a marauding army would overtake sectors of ground, making their way to their final objective.

This was when John was at his happiest—when he could serve as a patriarch to his men. His age and appearance made it easy for people to take direction from him. And his non-intrusive style of leadership had served him well in this outlaw world he had come to rule.

John knew Jack had most likely spent the night dealing with

Dave but said nothing except, "Hey, join us over here!" Of course, that did not stop John from observing Jack's hands and face for telltale signs of a confrontation.

After they had finished discussing the trip, John folded up the map. Robert asked if they needed to talk alone, preparing himself to check on the bikes. Jack shook his head. With a simple acknowledgment that it was great to see Dave, he assured John that things were good.

Jack also mentioned in passing that Brownie was still his same old self. This was good news for the old man because this was meeting night, and he planned to petition the club to put Jack in the number two spot behind him. John was still awkward with the term "president, " and now they were going to have a vice president, too.

How things had changed.

CHAPTER TEN

When they got back to the ranch, Jack and John made their way into the shop. It was time to get Jack's bike together. They had it laid out as if it was field-stripped for inspection, and one section of the shop was devoted to its re-assembly.

By the end of the day, as members gathered for the meeting, the flathead was no longer a skeleton of parts but had taken the shape of a custom-built bike. But John and Jack had to break for the meeting because it wasn't just another meeting. Rumors had been running wild among the membership that things were shifting. As uncomfortable as that was for some of the members, it was time to accept the truth. The meeting room was packed. John asked Robert, the only Question Mark prospect, to go check the bikes. Robert was sometimes allowed to sit in on meetings. So when he was asked to leave, it was a clear signal to everyone that something serious was about to be discussed.

As Robert made his way out, John started talking about what would become a defining night in the club's history.

From the back of the room, quiet Dick Woods spoke up in his low, gentle voice. Dick was a lean man, with thick blond hair pulled straight back, and a neatly trimmed beard that made him look as if he had just stepped out of a "B" biker movie. He was just a couple years younger than John and just as tough. Some in the club felt he was just as an important a figure, and the way John treated him seemed to confirm that. The old man and Dick had been the first to fly the soon-to-be, not just infamous, but also famous, Question Marks.

"Hey, John, can I speak?" asked Dick.

All attention was on him.

"You all know John, and I put this mob together, and I think we have come to a fork in the road. My better sense tells me if we don't bend some, we could break. All this media attention—biker movies, posters, newspapers—where did it begin and where will it stop? As much as I've been against it, we need more order. I want to propose John as president."

The room erupted into clapping and yells of approval.

Someone in the back yelled, "Dick should take the vice president spot."

John shifted uncomfortably in his chair. This wasn't what he had hoped for at all.

Dick raised his voice louder than he had in years. "I need you all to hear me out," he said. "What we need is young blood. And I think what the club needs right now is Jack."

John shot his old friend a thank-you look. Then, to everyone's surprise, Dave spoke up and seconded Jack. And with no one about to voice any objections from this overwhelming power of support, the new leadership was established.

The club was ready to meet its destiny.

Jack asked for the floor. He seized the moment to bring up Robert for full membership. The spirit in the room was high, and Jack felt he could get the 100 percent vote needed for a new member.

There were no objections until they got to the last member—Dave. With the smoke from his cigarette forming a cloud around his head, Dave said with a smile on his face, "I'm not sure he's ready."

This really wasn't about Robert. Dave obviously didn't want to appear weak to Jack or anyone else. But Jack sure as hell didn't want to get shut down in his first action as a leader.

Thinking on his feet, Jack took a political gamble. He knew how sore he was from the confrontation the night before and figured Dave was in similar shape.

"Well, if that's how you feel," Jack told Dave, "I think you should go outside and run him off."

This was a big risk because there was a good chance Dave would have done just that on any other night—but not this night. Dave smiled slowly before raising his hand to make the vote unanimous.

John finished the meeting talking about the upcoming trip to Sturgis. They called Robert back into the meeting and asked if he was ready to ride cross-country as a Question, Mark. He assured the members he was, and John and Dick helped him lay out his three-piece patch on his black leather vest.

Jack looked around the room. It would be the last time he would see complete harmony within the club.

It was proving to be a historic night for others, as well. Over at BET headquarters, Sergeant Sherman had set up a meeting of his own. Every BET member converged on the squad conference room with the exception of four men who made up two surveillance teams. Their job was to gather intelligence on each and every person who was at the ranch for the Question Mark meeting.

In the front of the conference room was a large easel showing a full-scale layout of the ranch. It also showed the two roads that were the only ways in and out, and two perfectly drawn red circles, which reflected the best vantage points with the least exposure. On this night, BET would do their best to keep this operation covert. Sherman didn't want to tip the Marks that BET was actively gathering information. A reel-to-reel tape machine sat on the table in front of the easel. On it was the voices of various Question Mark members ordering breakfast, but also discussing club business. Several weeks earlier, the sergeant had personally led a team into the Frontier Café. The team members who entered the old diner chose an abandoned electrical box to place their bug. They used a small drop mic with an external battery that would need to be replaced from time to time. This would pose no problem. The café was a mom-and-pop operation—security wasn't exactly tight.

Posing as GT&E phone company employees, BET members also installed a new outside locked box that housed a receiver and field recorder. Sherman knew that the best way to protect his bug was to not show his hand with the intelligence he was now intercepting.

And there was another reason to protect the bug. Local Judge Perrin had turned down a request for a warrant to record conversations that took place in the restaurant. But this would be just the first of many illegal BET operations.

The sergeant knew this was going to be a long process, and he was willing to wait as long as it took to build a solid case against Jack Crest and his band of criminals.

The next two weeks were devoted to preparing for the trek to Sturgis. John, Jack, and various Question Marks continued to meet at the Frontier Café each morning. BET members were not only disappointed but frustrated that the only topic of conversation was the upcoming cross-country journey.

As the tape rolled and BET team members sat listening to the stories of the road, Officer Cory asked the sergeant why the BET unit wasn't making the trip. Sherman sat lost in thought for a minute. When he came out of it, he told Cory they were going for a ride.

A former high school football star, Cory was an imposing figure which was taken seriously by anyone who interacted with him. His short-cropped blond hair seemed to rise with static as his temperament shifted during conversations with enemies as well as friends.

Cory and Sherman jumped into the all-black BET sedan to make a short trip north up the old El Camino Highway, which was now US Route 101. Route 101 was the same highway traveled by men using the name of God to destroy another culture many years earlier. Now BET was determined to destroy the Question Marks before its roots could take hold. It took about twenty minutes for the pair to reach

Ventura City Hall, which held the local courthouse, jail, and main sheriff's office. It was a beautiful building overlooking the Southern California beach city of Ventura—not a tourist town yet, but the city fathers had big plans for it that did not include outlaw bike clubs.

Sherman pulled up in front and parked in the red zone as he always did, right at the base of the large cement steps that led to the front doors of the courthouse. Sherman had been warned to park in back with the other units, but it was a BET unit car, and in Sherman's mind BET set their own rules.

As Sherman and Cory walked up the steps and entered the large doors of the courthouse, their street clothes set off by the custom BET jackets caught the eye of everyone they passed on the way to the chief's office.

All BET team members carried the compact Detonics .45 with their badges mounted on their black holster belts next to the weapon, for all to see. Sherman took it one step further. Inside his jacket, yet often visible, he had a Smith & Wesson Air Weight .38 mounted in a custom black leather shoulder holster that matched the custom sidearm holster. It was an impressive sight, no matter which side of the law you were on.

"Why didn't you tell me we had a meeting with the chief?" asked Cory.

Entering the chief's office, Sherman winked at Cory. "We don't. Let me do the talking." There would be no argument from Cory as most people on either side of the law feared the chief, and Cory was now nervous.

The chief's secretary, who had grown accustomed to the

sergeant's unannounced visits, looked up expectantly. But she was disappointed with Sherman's brusque treatment.

"I believe he's tied up," she curtly told Sherman.

Not one to miss the cold greeting, Sherman didn't miss a step. "If I was your boss, you'd be the one tied up."

Although blushing furiously, a grin split her face and she mumbled, "Promises, promises."

Cory had never seen this side of his boss, and it was obvious from what he had just witnessed that Sherman believed he was the prince of the city. However, around the Question Marks, he was unnerved and out of step. Cory thought more and more that a personal issue lay between the sergeant and the Question Marks, and he was determined to find out what it was. The two of them entered the office. The chief didn't even look up.

"What do you want, Sherman?"

The chief was a compact, dark complexioned, distinguished-looking older man. The walls of his office were covered with pictures of powerful men and newspaper headlines that spanned four decades of work. It was rumored the chief had saved Sergeant Sherman's life as a rookie and had continued to mentor him up the chain of command. People also said that the chief thought that since he had saved Sherman's life, he was now responsible for it.

"I need money, boss," Sherman said.

The chief looked over the top of his glasses.

"You remember Cory," the sergeant added. "One of my men."

"Not really, Sherman, but I'll pretend I do. Everybody wants money. What's your story?"

"Well, boss, we're really starting to make some headway out in Somis, and a reliable confidential informant has given us some intel that suggests something big is going to happen this year at Sturgis."

"How good is this information?"

"It's like I'm sitting at the same table with them," replied the sergeant.

The chief gave Sherman a dubious look and quit asking questions.

"Okay, I'll contact our man in Washington for some federal assistance."

"Does that mean they'll have to be there?"

"I would imagine they would. It's their money."

Sherman didn't look happy with that answer, and the chief added, "Your cooperation is necessary and expected, Sergeant. Is that understood?"

Addressing Sherman as "Sergeant" was the chief's way of letting him know he meant what he said, and Sherman answered him as a pouting son would answer a lecturing father.

The chief made good on his promise, and the funding was sent. The BET team was cleared for two team members to make the trip. But in clear defiance, Sherman added two more of his team members for the operation.

Cory was put in charge of logistics, including support weapons. It looked like BET had found their number-two man. As he inventoried the ammunition, Cory came across something in the ammo bag that left him with a sick feeling. It was a snub-nose, nine shot .22 pistol, carefully wrapped in a dirty white hand towel. What really caught his attention was the ground-off serial number. This was what was known as a "throw-down gun," used to explain shooting mistakes by officers as a way to cover their asses.

After inspecting the weapon, Cory wrapped the throw-down back in the towel, returned it to the bag, and zipped the bag up. He shut the trunk and headed back toward BET's rear door. But an errant thought struck him, and his knees weakened. Overwhelmed with concern, Cory stopped in his tracks and returned to the rear of the unit. He looked around, opened the trunk, and unzipped the bag. He reached in and located the weapon. He unwrapped it and then slowly and deliberately wiped off his prints. Then he carefully wrapped it back up and placed it right back where he had discovered it.

When he returned to headquarters, Sherman commented that Cory was sweating. Cory made a passing comment about the summer heat, but he could tell Sherman didn't buy it. He'd better watch his step.

BET was now ready to go.

Of course, it would be the Question Marks who set the pace across the United States.

It was bound to be an interesting trip.

CHAPTER ELEVEN

The ranch had been busy with Question Marks coming and going in preparation for the Saturday departure. In the middle of the shop sat Jack's 80-inch flathead. The scene around the bike resembled a maternity waiting room full of first-time fathers. It was Jack's bike, but just about all the members had put some time into it. It didn't matter what club or what part of the country, this same scene was played out over and over in shops and garages across the country. They were all bike riders, builders, and brothers. Jack could feel the camaraderie of this esoteric culture. How could outsiders ever hope to break this bond they didn't understand. It might all fall apart under the weight of money, power, greed, and fame, but that would be up to the club and members themselves, not outside forces.

Jack kicked life into the two cylinders, and the straight pipes echoed from wall to wall, silencing all conversation. Old Man John pointed the large fan into the motor to keep the temperature down. Dick let the oil run directly into a mason jar, bypassing the oil tank. After the jar had filled, Jack killed the motor. While the motor cooled, Dick passed around the jar of oil so everyone could see all the metal that had come out with the oil. They all nodded with approval as Dick spilled the oil into the pan.

He added three fresh quarts as Jack torqued every bolt he could reach. It was now ready for a break-in ride up the coast.

Jack mounted the bike, kicked it over, and was ready to ride. Robert was waiting to accompany his club brother. All eyes were on them, like parents watching their daughter on her first date, as they rode off into the setting sun. Jack had only a few days left to work out any bugs and put some miles on the new motor.

BET had continued to monitor the conversations at the restaurant. They determined that the Question Marks would be riding out on Saturday morning. The Marks had discussed several different routes, but the old man and Jack were the only ones who knew which one they would take.

Well, almost the only ones.

Sherman and his men knew Mesquite, Nevada, would be the club's first night stop, and they'd be there waiting.

John had borrowed one of the prop delivery trucks from Mr. Hayward to serve as the support vehicle. It was equipped with tools, an array of spare parts, and camping equipment. The old man was impressed with Jack's ability to organize, and he deferred everything to him. As the Saturday takeoff approached, more members arrived from the Bay Area. By Saturday morning it looked like they would leave the ranch with a pack of close to thirty bikes. They would also be picking Question Marks up from the south as they traveled east out Highway 15. Such a large pack would look like a hundred outlaw bike riders marauding their way across God's chosen land. The sound and the sight of this many bikes together would draw attention from the media, the public, and most certainly the law.

They left at 0500 sharp to get a jump on the desert heat.

John walked out to his bike and mounted it like a cavalry general would mount his horse. The excitement had been building all night, and the time had come. Members started mounting their bikes, but they all waited for the sound of John's pipes before they brought their iron horses to life.

They pulled out onto Highway 118 two abreast. Every hundred-mile gas stop added a few more members, and by the end of the day, the pack had swelled to near fifty as they pulled into Mesquite.

Though it would eventually become a resort town, Mesquite was little more than a truck stop, a restaurant with a bank of slot machines and a row of small rooms for truckers who didn't have sleepers in their cabs. Jack had called in advance so that the club had rooms for the night. It would be another early departure.

Las Vegas was eighty miles behind them, and the club skipped it as a stop by design, not chance. They had learned that the hard way.

The club's first trip across the country became a disaster when Vegas was picked for the first night's stop. By daylight, anyone who hadn't lost all their money gambling had lost it to ladies- of-the- night in one manner or another. Some members determined to continue on, waiting for the money to arrive by the Western Union. The rest of the crew returned home to a defeated army.

That was the first and last time Vegas was a stop.

Police radios and teletype were warning the masses of the impending doom. If the BET unit wanted to remain under the radar, they should have stayed in Ventura County, because from this day forward they would be the envy of many throughout law enforcement.

The irony was that many officers felt that at last, law enforcement had their own group of one-percenters to deal with these outlaw misfits on their own terms—fire with fire. This world was turning upside down, and at some point, Sergeant Sherman would have to accept that he and his BET team were only adding to the confusion. Earlier in the day, Sherman had taken a calculated guess that Victorville, California, would be the first gas stop.

He was right.

He had asked the San Bernardino County Sheriffs for a little professional courtesy, to assist BET with gathering intel on the large pack of Question Marks that would be invading the small town. Sherman asked to have the info waiting for the BET unit in Mesquite.

The Sheriff's Department not only rose to the occasion, but they also went above and beyond the call of duty by notifying every jurisdiction from Victorville to Mesquite that the Question Marks would be coming through.

By the time BET reached Mesquite, every cop in the town was waiting for them and overwhelming the BET four team members with first-class treatment.

Sherman split up his team and had them ride in local marked cars to gather any last-minute intelligence from the road. Although all the attention was intoxicating, Sherman had already made a decision to drive straight to Sturgis the next morning. He'd try to beat the rumors and reports that would soon be atop the desk of the Sturgis police chief.

Sherman was concerned that the attention would shift from the band of rebels heading their way, to rumors that soon there would be a new sheriff in town from California. If that happened, maybe the sergeant and his boys wouldn't have such a warm reception by their law enforcement brothers in Sturgis.

Jack was up at dawn. He had long ago developed the ability to set a time in his mind and wake up within a few minutes before or after. The night before, he had put all the prospects in one room so none of them would get lost, which seemed to happen often with prospects. He gave them all a pep talk on how, although they were from different areas, they were all Question Marks prospects.

After lifting their spirits, he passed out the night's watch list, something no one had ever done in the past. As Jack was exiting the small room, he heard some remarks that didn't sit well with him. He did an immediate about-face and scanned through everyone in the room.

"Is there a fucking problem?" he asked.

The room fell silent. Jack lingered long enough to stare down each and every one them.

By morning light, Jack told the last team of prospects who were still on watch duty to start waking up the members. "They have one hour to eat and gas," he instructed them.

John and Jack parked their bikes at the edge of the parking

lot and waited. Soon the lot was a sea of bikes. Eighty miles west, the Vegas metro organized crime unit was taking an interest in the large group of bikers about to move east.

Sergeant Jim "Jimmy" Jones. Close friends called him "Triple J." He could count those friends on the one hand.

Jones had been investigating organized crime in his hometown of Vegas for many years, and he was personally responsible for putting several mob figures in the infamous Black Book that could ban you from entering any casino in Nevada for life.

Jones felt that any Question Mark names would make a nice addition to the book if they ever had a notion of invading his hometown. Jones had followed the pack of bikes from a gas station at Whiskey Pete's at State Line. Every license number on every bike was recorded and entered into a spiral notebook. In addition, his officers took pictures of numerous members, shot with a high-speed camera behind tinted windows.

Metro put that afternoon's intelligence together and headed east to Mesquite, arriving around midnight. Anyone with a solid background in law enforcement could see the real reason for the trip: Jones needed to know if this BET team measured up to the standards of the Vegas organized crime unit.

Metro didn't know if they liked what they saw, but were willing to give BET a chance. It didn't take long for Sherman to figure this out and soon kicked the local Mesquite cops, who had nothing to offer, to the curb. He opted instead to accompany Metro in their high-tech van. Metro positioned the van at the far end of the lot, giving them the best observation point of the activity taking place at the motel.

The interior of the van was made comfortable to accommodate boring, extended periods of surveillance. Jones and Sherman sat in silence for a while, measuring each other up. Jones spoke first. "Lets cut the bullshit. Let me give you some professional advice." The Metro Sergeant explained that if this was intended to be a covert trip BET was making, it wouldn't be for long. Jones went on to explain that an all-black sedan with California plates was going to attract attention, not to mention the four men inside wearing BET jackets.

"Of course," he added, "I'm certainly not trying to offend the BET unit."

Sherman immediately replied, "But we're dealing with men who deny even the hint of being a structured organization, let alone engaging in criminal activity. We want to be an in-your-face unit."

"Well, maybe you can walk in both worlds," Jones said. "I have some things for you."

He handed Sherman a box. Inside were license plates from all over the United States, taken from cars at the Las Vegas police impound yard. Because Vegas was a vacation mecca, every few months, Metro would help themselves to any plates they needed.

He also gave Sherman the spiral notebook with all of the Question Mark license plate numbers, and several rolls of undeveloped film. Sergeant Jones extended his hand to Sherman. As they firmly shook, Jones said, "We're both after the same result."

The next several hours were filled with war stories from each unit and an exchange of opinions on how the Question Marks should be investigated. It was obvious to Jones that the Marks were a criminal enterprise with a clear chain of command.

Unconfirmed reports had eastern outlaw bike riders doing some work for crime families, and this was a good reason to start a program of information sharing. Cut this off before it spreads, Jones thought.

As the pack left the parking lot to start its day's ride east, Sergeant Jones vowed he would never allow outlaw bike riders in his town. Little could he dream that within ten years, three of the "big four" outlaw bike clubs would not only be crowding his town, but they would also openly be fighting for control.

The Question Marks were in an upbeat mood as they settled into their second day on the road. The local Mesquite cops followed them to the state line, a mile ahead. Once the bikes crossed into Arizona, the squad cars parked and watched the pack wind its way up into the virgin mountains of Arizona.

As the pack, fifty bikes strong started the ascent, members started breaking ranks. Then out of nowhere, several riders with handguns emptied them into the mountainside. Gypsy, a Question Mark out of Venice, California, stole the day when he un-slung his semi-automatic Uzi and emptied the magazine into a barrel cactus.

Jack shot a disapproving glance at the old man, who just shrugged his shoulders. Jack signaled with hand gestures to cut the gun play, and the riders refocused on the winding road surrounded on each side by breathtaking red mountain cliffs. They were deep in the Grand Canyon National Monument, and it was a sight to see.

It was a fast ride through the mountains, and coming out of

the pass Jack could see the Arizona-Utah border, with the city of St. George, Utah, in the distance. As they passed the truck scales at the state line, several Utah State Troopers were waiting near a line of cruisers. They ran to their vehicles as the pack crossed into their state.

The old man looked over at Jack and shook his head. They both tried to focus on the rear of the pack, but it was too long to clearly make out what was being reflected in the small vibrating bike mirrors.

Starting from the rear forward, each member tapped the top of his head, the hand signal for cops. The two lead bikes had to make a decision whether to stop for gas or wait out the cops by keeping the pack going east.

John tapped on his gas cap several times, and Jack put up his hand to signal they would be turning off. The first thing that came to Jack's mind was that Utah was a dry state, full of religious fanatics. Jack was sure this was going to become a standoff of sorts, and he prepared himself mentally for whatever hand the Marks were dealt.

He made a quick survey of the gas stations to find the one that would best serve their needs. He pointed out one to John that had it all: gas, repair shop, store, and drive-in style restaurant. It had lots of room for parking. The objective was always to contain your members in a single location and get back on the road within a reasonable amount of time.

They pulled into two different pumps and two pumps only. That way, there could be no dispute about the bill. Each morning, two prospects would gather ten dollars from each member for the day's ride. At a station stop, they'd have the attendant start the pump, and after the last bike was fueled, they'd pay the bill and get a receipt. This kept everyone honest.

John and Jack had the luxury of gassing up first and getting a parking place in the shade. John had made his way to the drive-in for a burger, while Jack stood by the bikes watching the state trooper units circle the surrounding streets like sharks.

When John walked back to Jack, the troopers made their move. They shot into the lot, and behind the cover of their units' doors, they asked who was in charge. Without missing a beat—and with a mouthful of food—John pointed at Jack. But the trooper caught Jack a little off-guard. "If I don't get some pictures with you guys," he said with a smile and a down-to-earth attitude, "my kids will never believe me."

They spent the next half hour taking pictures, talking bikes, and discussing the best routes to beat the speed traps. The locals came out, and all the participants had a damn good time.

The prospects left the surrounding area cleaner than when they arrived, and merchants told them to be sure to stop by again on their way back to California. Finally, everybody said their goodbyes. The Question Marks pulled out, and they were back on the road. The troopers even kept the lane clear until the pack once again got into a good tight formation. They waved their last goodbye as they crossed the highway to circle back toward St. George.

The rumble of the pack clocked down the mile markers on the side of the road, and Jack rode silently embarrassed that he had prejudged a whole group of people without ever having met them.

The next four stops in Utah were a repeat of the St. George experience.

The Question Marks had definitely made new friends in Utah.

CHAPTER TWELVE

Eastbound on I-70, the Question Marks roared across the next state line in their path. Welcome to Colorado. But all the "Kumbaya" moments they enjoyed in Utah came to a sudden halt; the Centennial State had a serious roadblock waiting. Colorado State Troopers had been watching from the air for miles. They were determined to send a message: Colorado doesn't like or want, one-percenters in their state.

Period.

As the pack neared the police units blocking the road, even more units fell in around and behind the motorcycles. As the units surrounded the bikes, the Question Marks were careful not to open any breaks in the pack that would allow the cops to separate them.

The pack slowed to a standstill, and the peace officers positioned themselves into a complete blockade of I-70, both ways. They also proudly displayed their standard-issue riot pump shotguns as a show of force. They made it clear that they were very armed and very ready.

However, they never directly pointed the weapons at anyone,

and that spoke volumes to Jack. Neither group wanted a real problem to come out of this encounter.

The Colorado State Troopers' sergeant who was heading things up looked young for his rank. Jack pinned him as ex-military. The sarge had no fear in his eyes or step. But Jack wasn't so sure about the rest of these cops who now had the core of the Question Marks surrounded in the middle of nowhere.

Jack spoke first, which the old man tacitly approved. "Why didn't you just wait till we got to Grand Junction? This is a cluster fuck, Sergeant."

"It may be," replied the kid-faced cop, "but it's my cluster fuck."

Jack handed the sergeant his license before he could ask for it, a psychological play to take back some control.

The sergeant inspected the license, then spoke. "We have two problems here, Mr. Crest. One is your speed, and the other is the Uzi slung over that rider's shoulder, for God and everyone to see."

Handing the license back to Jack, the young cop noticed the large USMC tattoo on the inside of Jack's right forearm. Jack took notice that he did.

"Sergeant," said Jack, "that weapon is a legal semi-automatic, and having it displayed in the manner it is, complies with all state and federal laws."

"It doesn't look good to the public," the sergeant came back with.

Both men were silent a moment.

"So how does this sound?" the sergeant proposed. "You bring

the weapon to me with the bolt open and no magazine. I will run the numbers, and if it comes back clear, you put it in the truck following you—at least until you leave Colorado."

"Sounds fair," Jack said. "And as to the speeding, there will be no more issues with that. You have my word." Jack extended his hand, and the sergeant shook it firmly.

Meanwhile, the freeway was now backed up a mile or so, and the other troopers were slowly letting the traffic pass. Their stop-and-go act added to the sergeant's cluster fuck. Car passengers had their cameras pointed out the window, and the Question Mark members were performing for their audience.

And the scene wasn't over yet.

Robert was now slowly swaggering his way to the front of the bikes, where the peace exchange was taking place between Jack, John, and the troopers. Robert had picked up a black leather riding whip somewhere in Utah to add to his all-black gear. It hung from his right wrist, and there was no question he was dressed to impress.

Robert extended his fingerless black-gloved hand to the young sergeant as Jack introduced them. That went well, but it was obvious to Jack that Robert was up to some mischief. Robert told the troopers that he liked their dark-colored uniforms and that their Smokey the Bear hats really set it off.

They let Robert know that his uniform was also quite impressive.

Jack and the old man exchanged glances, knowing it was coming soon.

"But I wonder something," Robert said to the sergeant. "Why do you troopers have your hats on backward?" All eyes went to the troopers' hats for an assessment. They all looked in order. But everyone now focused on the sergeant as he slowly raised his hand to the front center of the hat and felt for the silver emblem.

It was nowhere to be found. The sergeant had his hat on backward. He looked at Robert. "Why, thank you, Robert," he said dubiously.

Robert raised his whip to his forehead in a military-style salute. "Anytime, Sergeant." Then he disappeared to the rear of his bike.

"I think we're done here," the sergeant said awkwardly.

Old Man John took a puff of the cigar he'd been smoking on the road and spoke up. "Sounds good. I'd like to get to Grand Junction before dark."

"That's our stop for tonight," added Jack.

"We know," said the sergeant.

Grand Junction was just down the road and was planned as a major stop. It had a Harley shop in town, which would accommodate members who wanted to change their oil after the hard miles through the desert.

The motel layout was perfect. The manager gave them a bank of rooms in the back, and a family-style restaurant was connected to the motel parking lot. The staff seemed to enjoy these strangers from out West, and that made the food taste better than it really was. The Question Marks showed their gratitude with good manners and generous tips.

John and Jack could see the members were enjoying themselves. With a couple days of hard riding under them, they needed a little R&R. After going over the map, they set departure time for noon the following day. They would ride the 385 miles into Cheyenne, Wyoming, and be there by dark. That would put them only one day out from Sturgis.

Perfect.

Jack looked up to find Robert standing in the doorway of his room. Robert always puts a smile, if not on Jack's face, certainly in his heart.

"What the hell are you up to, brother?" asked Robert.

"I'm waiting for the old man to shower so we can grab some dinner. You look like you could use a meal. Want to join us?"

"Sounds good." Robert stripped the filter off his cigarette and packed the end with the roach of the joint he had smoked earlier in the day. He lit it and drew the smoke in, then he passed the last of the roach-filled cigarette to Jack. Jack drew it deep into his lungs and smiled at Robert.

While they waited for John, Robert took the opportunity to let Jack know he had done a hell of a job the last couple days. Robert told him he really had a way with people, and that included cops.

"Why, Robert," Jack replied, "Are you now considering cops people?"

Most likely from his past as a military brat, Robert had a real problem with figures of authority—especially cops.

"You know, those cops in Utah were far out. You think they

were Mormons?"

"How the hell would I know?"

"I'm just saying," said Robert, "I never met cops like that before. And them last cops, that could have got real ugly. I'm not talking shit, but the old man seems like he's getting tired."

Feeling the flare of anger, Jack told Robert, "I hope you're not talking shit because he built this mob and as far as I'm concerned it will always be his."

Robert came back fast. "No, no, no—don't misunderstand. What I'm saying is he needed you, and it was cool. It was you that was there for him. It's a good thing."

John walked out the bathroom. "What are you two hoodlums up to?"

Stifling a laugh, Jack explained, "Well, this trip is really expanding Robert's horizons. He even found some cops he likes." They all had a good chuckle and started making their way to the restaurant. As they passed each room, they picked up bits and pieces of conversations. Everyone was in high spirits.

Smokey and Gypsy had a poker game underway, which would most likely last until they pulled out tomorrow.

John asked the waitress to seat them at a table at the rear of the restaurant, where they could talk. Jack and Robert exchanged a puzzled glance.

After the waitress had brought three beers and three shots of tequila, the old man offered up the neck of his beer bottle in a toast. As Robert and Jack raised their beers, the three objects became one for a brief moment. The old man looked Jack and Robert deep in their eyes and exclaimed, "Question Marks!" His words echoed around the table.

When the bottles were put back on the table, Jack eyed John. "You didn't bring us here in the back just for a toast." It wasn't a question.

"I know," John admitted. "I have something I want to say, and I need for you two to just listen. It's important that you hear what I am saying."

With that, John went on to explain, "No one knew this would all spread across the country like it has. We're moving east, and the Orphans are coming west. At some point, our two worlds are going to collide. Me—I'm an old scooter tramp—"

"This isn't what I signed up for," Jack interrupted. "You are the club." The Question Marks didn't have a national leader, and the old-timers liked it that way. But no one would deny that Old Man John had become the de facto voice for them.

"You need to hear me out, Jack," said John. "I'm tired and, honestly, this will soon be over my head." These were hard words for Robert to hear as well, but he understood better than Jack. There were fewer emotions in it for him.

"Dick and I started this, and I told him today what I am telling you and what I'll be telling all our brothers at the national meeting when we get to Sturgis. This will be my last trip cross-country."

Jack asked point-blank if the old man was done. John didn't speak but nodded yes. "Nothing has to change," Jack said. "You're going to lead us 'til the end."

John slowly shook his head. Quietly he said, "This is the end."

Just then the waitress made her way to the table, plates stacked in each arm. She passed the dinners out and was quickly gone, obviously sensing the heavy energy at the table. John went on with what he had to tell them, that he felt Jack should fill his spot and that Robert would fill that second spot nicely if he grew up a bit.

The men ate in silence for a while, each lost in his own thoughts. In the midst of his steak, Robert casually asked, "What if I don't wanna grow up?" They all broke into laughter, and the mood lightened.

But Jack noticed that John's eyes had become misty. Jack also knew that the old man's mind was made up. This subject was closed.

CHAPTER THIRTEEN

Morning came fast and John's words from the night before were sinking in. Jack began taking complete control of things—lighten the load for the old man on this trip; it'll help him to come to his senses.

That didn't happen. In fact, it just cemented the decision.

It was close to noon when Robert emerged from his room with a dancer he had picked up at the local strip club the night before. As Jack surveyed things, he saw that several members now had young ladies with them, and it was obvious they were now part of this caravan to South Dakota. Jack called Robert over. "What are you guys going to do when the run is over, and all these girls are a thousand miles from home?" he asked.

"I figured we would just drop them off on our way back."

"Well, you're riding with me, and we're not going home this way."

"Okay," Robert replied. "How does this sound? We'll get you a girl, and we can take them both back to California."

"And then what?" Jack asked. "No thanks!"

Robert's face became almost childlike. "You know, Jack," he said, "I think I might be in love..."

"Jesus Christ!" Jack exclaimed, "This is your idea of growing up?"

Robert shot back, "I told you last night, I'm not ready yet. And I'm sorry boss. You won't even know she's with us."

Jack just turned and walked away, mumbling, "Okay, okay."

"Thanks, boss!" Robert replied, returning to the waiting members—and women—with a smile on his face. "Let's go to Sturgis!" he told them.

Everyone was making last-minute adjustments for the road when David Brown's lowered black Cadillac pulled into the parking lot. Brownie and the other Dave were both in the back seat. Dave's old lady, Darcie, was at the wheel. She gave all the new girls the once-over as she cruised by. One of Darcie's girlfriends was asleep in the front passenger seat.

It was quite an entrance.

Old Man John looked at Jack and laughed. Brownie still had the bent rods in his legs and made no attempt to vacate the backseat as Dave stumbled into the parking lot with a crazed look in his eyes, declaring, "We came incognito." Brownie's medical issues had afforded him, and anyone around him an endless supply of pain meds, and both Brownie and Dave were taking full advantage of the drugs.

The old man was thankful Dave had not ridden with the pack but didn't miss the opportunity to let anyone within hearing distance know how he felt. "Like I said, I'm getting too old for this."

Jack replied back for everyone to hear, "You all look like a rolling felony!"

This new arrival aside, Jack asked John if they were sticking to their schedule. John answered by starting his bike. Within seconds, the pack roared back onto the I-70 east.

Dave stood staring in anger as the four of them were left alone in the parking lot. Darcie spoke up, testing the waters of Dave's temper. "Fuck 'em!" she said. "I didn't want to roll with them anyway."

Dave replied pretty much as expected as he watched the last bike speed onto the highway. "Shut up, Darcie!"

The main pack wouldn't see the Cadillac and its occupants again until they hit Sturgis. It was probably best for all parties concerned to have that time to cool down.

It was a fast climb into the mountains of Colorado. Off in the distance, patches of snow still dotted the landscape. It was a sight some of the California boys had never been this close to.

The river that skirted the highway looked wild and was moving fast as it flowed from one side, under the road, and crest on the other side. John and Jack kept the pack at a slower speed so they all could take in the beauty. The serenity was interrupted from time to time by a sheriff or trooper running from the back of the pack to the front writing down plate numbers and calling them in. This exercise became standard procedure as the pack moved from jurisdiction to jurisdiction. But no other roadblocks or hassles rose up to ruin the scenery.

They rolled into Denver on I-70 and then took I-25 north to Cheyenne, Wyoming. It was a fast day of riding with the exception of a few bikes having carburetor problems due to the higher elevation. The thinning air changed the mixture of the fuel sucked in by the big twin motors. But it didn't take the members long to troubleshoot and fix with some minor adjustments.

The Question Marks moved quickly down the highway. The pack had been on the road for three days and had found their center. They now moved as one. The sun was still high in the sky when they reached Cheyenne.

The motel they picked for the night was nice, the food in the restaurant was cheap, and the waitresses were all smiles. Jack told the members to take advantage of the light and get their bikes in order for the early morning departure time that he and John had set. Tomorrow they would be turning off the Interstate, rolling onto State Highway 85 North, just above Cheyenne. That two-lane road would slow their pace down as they passed through the small western towns of Wyoming.

They had been at the motel less than an hour when the first state trooper pulled into the vacant lot across the street. He parked but remained in his car. Of course, that didn't sit well with the Marks. They petitioned John to do something.

John's old-school response was not what they were looking for. "Well, they have their side of the street, and we have ours."

Jack saw that some type of response was expected and needed. He told John he would check it out, which took a little of the pressure off the old man, who was having a rough time with the heat and humidity. Jack reached into his saddlebags and pulled out his field glasses. He positioned himself in the parking lot directly across from the trooper. He raised the glasses and made no attempt to hide what he was doing. He could clearly see that the trooper had a set of binoculars of his own. The cop was resting them on the top of the steering wheel in an effort to keep them steady and get a clearer view of what was taking place at the motel. Jack and the trooper were now looking at each other through the field glasses.

Jack slowly took his right hand off the glasses, held up his palm to the trooper and wiggled his fingers in a tongue-in-cheek wave. He wasn't sure if it was a smile or a smirk that formed on the lips of the trooper, but Jack decided to venture over to the cruiser anyway.

The trooper exited his unit and positioned himself behind his door with his hand resting just above his revolver.

"What can I do for you?" he asked Jack. At the trooper's tone, Jack stopped short of the unit. "I wanted to let you know what we're doing," Jack told him.

The trooper responded again in a tone that was hard to read, "Hang on for a minute. My captain is a couple minutes away, you can tell him."

As Jack waited, he wondered if he had made a tactical error and should have stayed on "his side of the street," as John had put it.

The captain pulled in the lot, chauffeured by a young trooper who looked very scared. Behind the captain's unit was a pickup pulling a trailer. Jack instinctively knew this was a portable command post. Now five state troopers and a command post stood in what was a completely vacant lot just a few minutes before.

And they weren't finished yet.

The next to arrive were local peace officers. But the State Trooper captain was definitely in charge. His first words to Jack were a command: "You need to tell them to go back across the street."

He was referring to the Question Marks who had started to cross the street in order to back Jack up if there was a problem. Jack looked over his shoulder and raised his hand up to stop the forward movement of his club brothers. But he was happy they were close by.

"Now, what's on your mind?" the captain asked.

"I could ask you the same thing," retorted Jack. "This is a lot of attention for some people just passing through town."

"Well, you Question Marks have a terrible reputation."

"Yes, yes we do," replied Jack, "and we worked hard for it."

Silence.

It was a standoff until the captain finally spoke. "So, you're leaving in the morning?"

Jack replied, "First thing."

The captain had another question, "Which road will you be taking?"

As a Marine, Jack had lots of experience dealing with men in positions of leadership, and he immediately knew this was a man not to be trusted.

"I don't know yet, captain," he told him, "but that's what I love about this country."

Jack let the thought hang in the air until the captain pressed, “And what’s that?”

Jack’s answer was really a metaphor for what he saw was going wrong in the United States. He had just spent several years serving his country and had killed for the cause of freedom. The return home to a cold reception he could live with, but all of this police interest was not sitting well with him.

“Freedom of choice,” Jack replied.

The two men stared at each other until Jack reiterated that they’d be gone in the morning. And with that, he returned to the club members who had been anxiously waiting on the opposite side of the street.

“What a waste of money,” Jack said in passing.

He led the members back to the motel. He told the prospects to cut down the watch to one person because the troopers would be across the street until they pulled out in the morning.

Jack went back to the room to explain to the old man what was going on. The wrinkles in John’s face were full of worry. In all his years of riding as an outlaw, he had never encountered this much interest from either the police or the public.

“Fuck them,” was John’s response to all the information Jack shared with him. “We’ll be far from here and in South Dakota by noon tomorrow anyway.”

Jack sat in silence, pondering John’s statement. He realized for the first time that the old man really was out of step, out of his element with all of this attention. This was not the nineteenth century, and they weren't the James Gang who could cross a state line to evade arrest. What the old man had told Jack and Robert back in Grand Junction had been hard to swallow, but now the reality was sinking in more and more.

As the pack pulled out in the morning, the troopers stayed a reasonable distance behind but made sure all were aware of their presence. It didn't take long to reach the Highway 85 junction, and it was a relief to see the troopers continue north on I-25. The new highway was in good shape, but with only two lanes, the pack traveled at a slower pace than they had for the last three days. Passing through the small towns, the large procession of colorful choppers seemed almost parade-like.

Each town brought more people waiting on the streets for this odd sight to pass by. Some of the people waved, and the outlaws waved back. Young boys rode their bicycles up and down the sides of the pack at the stop signs, and some even tried to keep up as the motorcycles once again started their momentum forward. It was obvious the club members were enjoying the attention, but it put Jack in a pensive state of mind. His gut told him that law enforcement was alerting each one of these small towns that the pack was headed their way.

And the word was spreading.

Approaching the town of Lusk, Wyoming, Jack gestured to the old man that they should gas up and eat. John nodded his approval, and they pulled the pack into a good location where they could do both.

Adults and children kept coming by for a glimpse of these last American outlaws, and the Marks were enjoying every second of it. After about twenty minutes, a local sheriff's unit pulled in and parked, obviously assessing the situation.

The sheriff opened his door and, as he exited, the unit rocked from side to side. He looked to be at least six-foot-three with lean, long muscles and broad shoulders. His revolver was in a simple brown holster on his left hip, with the butt facing out. This would allow him to draw his weapon with either hand. Perhaps a modern quick draw, Jack thought.

Jack's first impression was that this man should be taken seriously. And he knew—as a man responsible for taking another man's life—that it was a good idea to avoid confrontation at almost any cost.

The sheriff kept his distance, but advanced close enough for the group to hear him ask who was in charge. Everyone looked at John and Jack. The old man pointed at Jack. Jack walked slowly toward the sheriff, who extended his hand in what seemed a genuine gesture. As they firmly shook, he introduced himself as Sheriff Perry. Jack returned in kind, and as a courtesy introduced himself with his full name. In a slow and deliberate voice, Perry told Jack he needed to ask him a couple questions if he didn't mind.

"Well I don't know if I can help, but what's on your mind, Sheriff?"

"How long you think you will be here in Lusk?"

"Just long enough to eat and gas, then we'll be on our way."

"Well, I wanted to ask a favor of you."

Surprised at the turn of the conversation, Jack asked, "What kind of favor would that be?"

"Well, you don't know, but I'm in the middle of a tough election." The sheriff made a quarter turn to the right and pointed out a huge billboard. "That's my deputy, gunning for my job." The billboard displayed a large headshot of a deputy, and in big block letters below it, "STEP INTO THE FUTURE—Elect Deputy Sheriff Larry Tanner!"

"If I thought he could do a better job, I might step aside. But Tanner's a bit of an asshole if you ask me, and stupid to boot. But he's also the mayor's son-in-law."

Jack chuckled. "So are you looking for an endorsement, Sheriff? Really, I don't think our support will help."

The sheriff laughed softly before replying. "I'm thinking more along the lines of an indirect endorsement. What I would like to do is after you guys leave town, if it's okay with you, I would like to say I ran you guys out of here. I think that will give me just the edge I need."

Jack laughed. He had to hand it to this guy. "Sheriff, if you think it'll help, once we leave town, tell them whatever you want."

The sheriff once again extended his hand. As they shook, he told Jack that it was downright kind of him. Jack returned to his brothers and explained what had transpired. The Sheriff gave a parting wave as he disappeared into the distance. Within the hour, the Question Marks were once again heading north to Sturgis.

The pack traveled the country backroads. In the private thoughts that go through the head of every serious rider, Jack tried to sort out the exchange he had just had with the sheriff, but he reached no conclusion. Soon, the sounds of the highway were the only thing that filled his head, and that suited him just fine.

CHAPTER FOURTEEN

The pack pulled into Sturgis at midday—right on schedule—riding straight to the campground. But as they parked at the entrance, the uneasy feeling Jack got from time to time once again set in.

And he didn't like it.

John had again deferred to Jack to deal with getting the club situated at the campground. Jack didn't know the camp manager and had only spoken with him a couple times about the arrangements. Now, face to face, the guy seemed very nervous. He kept glancing out at the sea of Question Mark patches flooding the parking lot and spilling into the small office drinking up the complimentary coffee and eating the donuts. One of the Question Marks from the Bay Area asked if there would be free beer and sandwiches later. All of which only added to the manager's stress as tried to explain to Jack that there had been a "mix up" and he was going to have to put them in a different area than the one Jack had reserved. The attendant spread out a map of the campground on the office desk to show Jack where the Marks would now have to camp.

But something else on the desk caught Jack's attention. His

anger rose as he decided to first make sure his eyes had not deceived him.

“Give me the map!” Jack demanded. He raised the campground map in front of him, but at an angle that gave him a clear view of Sergeant Sherman’s BET business card. Jack didn’t mention the card or even look at it again. In fact, he covered the card with the map as he threw it back on the desk.

“This won’t work,” declared Jack.

The attendant protested, “But what about the reservations I’ve been holding?”

“What do you mean, reservations you’ve been holding?” countered Jack. “You gave away our reservations.”

The old man met Jack as he left the office. “What’s wrong?”

“That motherfucker Sherman was here.”

“What are you talking about?”

“I saw his fucking card lying on the desk!”

“Fuck him and fuck this campground. Let’s roll.”

The members milling around could see something was wrong, and they huddled around John and Jack. “We’re leaving,” Jack told everyone. “I’ll explain later.”

Some of the members looked at John, who nodded in compliance. The pack rode up the highway about a mile and parked in an effort to regroup. Jack and the old man were in deep conversation by the time the members had assembled around them. What they had to say was for members’ ears only, and they made sure that any non-members retreated beyond hearing distance.

Jack explained what had happened in the campground office, and no one disagreed with his decision to move to a new location. Lots of suggestions were thrown out, but the majority agreed with Jack's plan.

They would go west to Bella Fourche, about twenty miles away, just east of the Wyoming state line. Jack figured that even though the locale would not stop BET, maybe it would slow them down. They sent a prospect back to the entrance of the campground to pass the word to the East Coast arrivals and any West Coast stragglers. North of Spearfish and well off the Interstate, the little town had always missed out on the Sturgis tourist trade. The people there were ready to welcome anyone to their town. Jack negotiated for an entire motel at a rate not much higher than the campground in Sturgis.

The Question Marks from the East thundered in just before dark, representing Nebraska, Kansas, Missouri, and Iowa. Their pack was good-sized, and they had something with them the West Coast didn't—more potential Question Mark club members.

The Eastern brothers brought the Saints From Hell, a solid-looking club out of Indiana, with charters in Indianapolis, South Bend, and Fort Wayne. They had been around for about ten years, and with close to fifty members they had earned respect in the one-percenters' world by owning their state.

They also had something important in common with the Marks: their dislike of the Orphans Motorcycle Club. The Saints were surrounded by the Orphans, who dominated the neighboring states. The fact that the Saints had managed to keep them out of

Indiana was a testimony to their tenacity.

After the new arrivals said their hellos and completed the introductions of the Saints, Jack's eyes fell on the prospect he had left at the campground entrance in Sturgis.

"What are you doing here?" Jack asked, keeping his voice neutral.

Before the prospect could reply, Silent Bob spoke up. Bob was to the Question Marks of the East what Old Man John was to the West, but much younger. He had helped shape and guide the East into the future. Standing tall and lean, he looked a cross between an old-school biker and a mountain man. He wore jeans that could be described as "originals," never to see soap or water. Over time, they'd been held together by dirt and oil. His vest matched his pants, and on the rare occasions that he did change into a new set, he would do them at the same time to keep his outfit in balance.

He set everything off with a pair of dirty, double-soled, suede cowboy boots. From time to time, he would shave the left side of his head to show off the Question Mark insignia tattooed above his left ear. He got his name, Silent Bob because once you got him started in a conversation, you couldn't shut him up. It looked like this would be one of those times.

"Ya see, Jack, that was my idea for him to come here. I sent some bros up to Gunner's Bar, and they heard rumors flying that we left town 'cause the Orphans are posted up in Rapid City. We saw a big pack pass us at a gas stop, and they didn't have no old ladies with 'em, and they were a war pack. I didn't want to have the prospect caught short, so I thought I'd better take him with us. Don't be mad at him, he did what he was told. Christ, Jack, we couldn't leave him there."

Jack raised his hand and said, "That's fine, Bob, you did the right thing. We have a meeting in the morning. We can sort this all out then."

Jack had found an old hall and rented it out for the morning meeting. He posted a couple of prospects outside for the night to ensure that BET would not find its way into the place beforehand.

The activity at the motel slowly subsided as the members and guests found their way to their rooms. Silent Bob was right: rumors back in Sturgis where running wild. Gunner's Bar on Main Street was the longtime hub for all the outlaw clubs and independent outlaw riders—if they were tough enough to stand on their own. The Orphans in Rapid City had sent a couple of people into Gunner's to see if they could find out why the Question Marks had pulled out. The word was now out that they had moved to Bella Fourche—but the question was why?

The Orphans weren't the only ones who needed some answers.

BET was in the campground office wanting answers of their own. Sherman came down hard on the attendant, pushing him with a series of accusations. He slammed his fist down on the desk.

"What the fuck went wrong? What did you say that spooked him?"

The attendant tried to explain that the change in camp location had angered the club member and he'd just walked out. Sergeant Sherman said they would be back for the surveillance equipment and if it was missing or damaged, he was holding the attendant financially responsible. In addition, if BET found out he had alerted anyone, they would be pursuing obstruction, perjury, conspiracy, and any other goddamn charge they could think of. With that, the four BET members stormed out of the office.

When they got into their cruiser, Sherman pounded his fist on the dash. "Son of a bitch," he thundered. "I'm gonna have some explaining to do when our friends from Washington arrive."

As Sergeant Sherman vented his anger in the campground parking lot, the lowered black Cadillac from California rolled up unnoticed by the BET team. The sight of an unmarked cop unit sitting in the campground parking lot alarmed everyone inside the Caddie. They decided to quickly and quietly continue on.

"Check that out," called out Dave, who was now driving, to Brownie who was still in the back.

"Fucking pigs," slurred Darcie from the passenger seat to anyone who would listen.

"We need more liquor!" proclaimed Amber, Darcie's girlfriend, who was in the back with Brownie.

The group had partied across seven states and had no plans to stop now. But they had tired of drinking from warm whiskey bottles and wanted a real drink from a glass. Dave headed to Gunner's to get it.

The Orphan lookouts in Gunner's Bar had called back to Rapid City to get the word to Orphan leader "Jimbo" that there were no Question Marks at the bar or in town. Jimbo weighed out the situation and made the decision to send a small group of Orphans to Gunner's so everyone in Sturgis could see they were there, and that the Question Marks were not. Jimbo had employed the tactic for years. The Orphans would ride into events with no colors and then appear out of nowhere. Some called it cowardice; others called it guerrilla warfare and had a reserved respect for its employment.

When Dave and Brownie strolled into Gunner's, they were greeted as returning heroes, which their women seemed to love even more than the two Question Marks did. They were the first members from any of the major bike clubs to come into the town. The independent riders liked it when the Question Marks were around because they had a reputation for treating people with respect. Their presence also kept the other bike clubs in check, and this made them mythic heroes to many in the bike culture.

The Orphan's lookouts were briefly at a loss as to their next move. They knew that jumping on the pay phone could alert Dave and Brownie, who had positioned themselves at the back of the bar against a wall with a clear view of the front and rear exits.

The lookouts decided they would wait for the right time, and one would go out front to smoke and warn any unsuspecting Orphans who arrived. The Question Mark's table was now covered with rounds of drinks bought by patrons in the bar. As Darcie and Amber danced together, Brownie turned to Dave and asked, "What are you thinking?" The situation sobered them both up a bit, but they continued to sip their drinks.

"I say we're here and they aren't." They both knew he was referring to the Orphans. They sat silently, deep in thought and observation. The music was loud, but as the front door opened the noise of a small pack of bikes echoed inside.

Five Orphans parked in front of the bar, flying their colors for all to see.

The lookout passed the word to the first Orphan rider to hit the sidewalk and then disappeared back into the bar. The crowd parted as the Orphans entered Gunners. The members were loud and crude, but they were not dumb. They were about ten years behind the Question Marks in outlaw evolution but had moments of brilliance over the years.

To diffuse the tension that was building, the Orphans member who entered first made his way to the bar. He was being vocal, but not aggressive. He made his way to the Question Marks and asked if they had seen any Saints From Hell members.

"Who wants to know?" asked Dave.

"Joy Boy," the man answered back. "Orphans MC."

Darcie and Amber had returned to the table, and Darcie burst into laughter. "What kind of fucking name is that?"

Joy Boy immediately backhanded her as he bellowed out, "Check your woman!"

Before Joy Boy had even finished his sentence, Dave was out of his chair delivering an upward head-butt under the Orphan's chin. Joy Boy's mouth slammed shut, splitting open his tongue. The blood gushing from his mouth made it look much worse than it was. Before the injured biker had time to react, Darcie was on his back with her legs wrapped around his waist. She held the back of his hair with her left hand and stabbed him repeatedly in the shoulder with her right.

She had pulled the Buck knife out of somewhere and with a one-handed flick of the wrist had put the blade to work.

Dave gazed proudly at his woman for a split second, until he was rushed by two more Orphans. The first Orphan threw his best punch, connecting with Dave's chin. Dave stood his ground and gazed deeply into the Orphan's eyes. With a smile, he asked, "Is that all you got, big boy?"

Dave slammed the guy into the nearest wall, and everyone could hear the air leave his lungs. Before Dave could let go, the next Orphan was on him, screaming "Motherfucker!" as he grabbed the back of Dave's hair with his left hand and Dave's chin with his right hand.

But the Orphan made a fatal mistake in his effort to manipulate Dave's head. His right thumb slipped into Dave's mouth. Like a pit bull in a dogfight, Dave bit down to the bone.

The Orphan screamed in agony. Dave spun off the wall and turned around to deliver alternating blows to his opponent's head, all the time continuing to bite down on the thumb.

The other two Orphans rushed Brownie and grabbed him, the bigger Orphan demanding he stands and fights. Brownie wanted to do that more than anything, but there was no way he could accommodate them. Fortunately, he had his long-barrel western revolver concealed in his vest. As the Orphans pulled and tugged at him, Brownie slid it out in one motion and pistol-whipped the Orphan who had demanded he rise. The Orphan, whose face was now laid open, jumped back in surprise.

The Orphan next to him yelled, "He don't get no bullets!"

At that, Brownie cocked the hammer and shot between them. Whether the missed shot was intentional was beside the point.

The Orphan screamed out, comically, "He's got bullets! He's got bullets!"

As the bar cleared, Amber, who had never seen anything like this, stood by frozen until Brownie screamed at her to help him up. They left through the rear door, but Dave had to come back to grab Darcie, who was now kicking any remaining Orphans unfortunate enough to be left in the bar. They ran out of Gunner's into the night.

No one had called the police, but the Sturgis cops along with BET were now at Gunner's. They would come away empty because nobody in this center of the outlaw world was about to talk to cops.

It didn't take long for Sherman to see they were wasting their time. This was the second time today he had struck out and was now more determined than ever to make the trip productive.

The Orphans made their way back to Rapid City. Some were in need of medical care, but all knew that a visit to an emergency room would bring police interest—which wouldn't sit well with Jimbo. They also had some explaining to do when they hit camp. As Orphan "Doc" worked on them, they each slowly told their story.

Doc had been an Army Corpsman and always had a medical bag close by, which had served the club well over the years. The story they told had been agreed on before they even hit town. There was no way Joy Boy or any other Orphan was going to admit to being beaten down by one man, one cripple, and a woman.

They all told Jimbo that it was obviously a trap, that the Marks had staged the exit to Belle Fourche to draw them in.

"We got set up."

Jimbo was not a trusting man and listened to the story with much reservation. He got up without saying a word and left.

Dave and Brownie thought this would be a good time to join their brothers. They knew they had to answer for what had happened and wanted to get it behind them sooner rather than later. When they found the rest of their crew, they woke up John and told him there had been a problem in town. They went to Jack's room where Old Man John, Jack, Dick Woods, and Silent Bob listened as they described the fight in Gunner's. What they told the room was almost exactly what had happened. Lying to a brother was a kick-out offense for a Question Mark.

Jack spoke first. "Brownie, you need to get that gun powder off your clothes and hands." Then he turned to Dave. "Did Darcie get rid of the knife?"

"She washed it real goo—"

Jack interrupted. "No, that's not good enough. Get rid of it."

"But it was a gift." They all broke into laughter.

Dave said to Jack, "You gotta tell her. I don't feel like fighting her tonight."

Bob Ingram and Bill Bradley had taken the red-eye from Washington D.C. to Rapid City for the intelligence meeting at the Sturgis Police Department Headquarters. Sergeant Ames of the Rapid City Police Department Intelligence Unit picked them up at the airport. Ames had a history with the feds through his work gathering intelligence on AIM, the American Indian Movement.

Because Sturgis was a small community, the overflow of outlaw riders had bled into Rapid City. Community leaders concerned about what they saw as a potential threat to their summer tourist trade had petitioned local law enforcement. When Ames was asked to attend the meeting in Sturgis, the Rapid City P.D. saw it as an opportunity to appease the city fathers and get them off their backs.

When the three men arrived at the Sturgis Police Headquarters, Sherman was standing out front. Seeing Ames with the two feds, Sherman felt like he had just been stood up at the prom. He quickly regained his composure, and in an attempt to gain control, the only BET member he allowed into the meeting was Cory. After an awkward introduction to Ames, they all entered the police headquarters.

The meeting was made up of the five men who had just entered the building, Detective Lt. Ames (the brother of Sergeant Ames), Chief Hagerty who like many small-town police chiefs sometimes worked in the field as a street officer, and a pensive ATF officer already seated in the room and introduced only as "Scott."

As things got underway, a man joined the meeting looking thoroughly out of place. He looked as if he had just walked off a ranch. He was tall and lanky. His brown hair could have used a cut, and he hadn't shaved in several days. His black cowboy boots were scuffed and in desperate need of new heels.

He pushed his cowboy hat back on his head and removed his worn denim jacket to reveal a wrinkled blue work shirt with a badge that said "Sheriff."

He wore no sidearm.

Bella Fourche Sheriff Will Cody had been invited as an afterthought, now that the Question Marks had "taken over" his town. He started by asking for a coffee. Once it was in his hand, he asked, "Well, gentlemen, what can I do for you?" They all looked at Cody as if he were in the wrong place, which, in all truth, he was.

Chief Hagerty made the proper introductions, then Bob Ingram took the floor. His pitch wasn't prepared, but he presented it well.

The essence of the meeting was that this was a special team with a special purpose: to cut out cancer spreading across the country, by any means necessary. Ingram didn't take long to make clear that the Question Marks were the target of the investigation and that the trophy would be the club's heir apparent, Jack Crest.

Ingram went on to explain that Scott, who represented the ATF, was the handler for someone who was now deep undercover in the outlaw world. The undercover operative's identity would only be revealed on a need-to-know basis. All he could share at this point was that the targets were specifically the Question Marks.

"Just what are these boys up too?" Sheriff Cody interrupted Ingram's speech.

"We aren't sure yet," Ingram replied.

Then Cody asked, "Is it what they're doing or how they're living?"

"It's both," Scott interjected.

"That doesn't sound like a crime to me."

"Well, we're not done yet," replied Scott with a tinge of sarcasm.

The conversation clearly wasn't going as Ingram had planned.

"Look, we're just trying to extend you a little professional courtesy," he told Cody.

Will Cody looked around the room, taking the time to make eye contact with each and every person. Then he spoke. "It sounds to me like you boys are on a fishing expedition. And I do my fishing on my days off. I need to get back to Bella Fourche. I have police work to do." And with that, he thanked them for the coffee and excused himself.

Ingram called out to him. "I hope this will remain confidential."

"Oh, believe me—it will," Cody replied. "I really wouldn't want anyone to know I was ever here."

The meeting didn't accomplish anything and ended abruptly. The Ames brothers took the opportunity to catch up—they hadn't seen each other in a long while. Chief Hagarty went back to his own duties. Ingram, Cory, and Sergeant Sherman discussed the sudden exit of the Question Marks to Bella Fourche, contemplating if Sheriff Will Cody's attitude somehow showed a connection to these renegades of society. Agent Scott and Bill Bradley spoke quietly in the corner, consumed with their own covert agenda.

The Question Marks' meeting started on time. It had been a year since they had all gotten together, and they had some open issues to vote on. As he had done year after year, Old Man John served as meeting chairman, while Dick Woods called himself a referee, since he didn't like the title Sergeant-at-Arms.

Dick called the meeting to order and took roll call. John apologized for the last-minute change of venue and deferred to Jack for the explanation. Jack detailed his suspicions that the campground security had been compromised. No one was going to complain anyway; they all liked the new accommodations. In fact, the motel spoiled everyone. In the future, "roughing it" would mean a motel without room service.

Jack went on to tell the members an incident had occurred with the Orphans the night before at Gunner's. He was purposely vague about the details and the people involved, though he didn't explain why. The smarter members knew that this was to protect the Question Marks involved. The details would remain on a need-to-know basis.

Jack got another one of his gut feeling that the incident wasn't over—with the Orphans or the BET team. He felt awkward about escalating the conflict because they were halfway across the country from their home turf. When they rode home, the Orphans would be left in the hands of the eastern Question Marks.

But Silent Bob made it clear that the brothers from the east had had enough of the Orphans and didn't care who started last night's shit in Gunner's bar. Both John and Jack respectfully shut down Silent Bob, concerned that he would reveal the details and players in his emotional state of mind.

It was decided after the meeting adjourned, that the Question Marks would head to Main Street in Sturgis in one large pack. Nobody objected. The members were itching to engage the Orphans.

This presented the perfect opportunity to open the topic of the proposed membership of the Saints From Hell. The Saints were very well liked and respected by the Question Marks, and voting them in would send a clear message to the Orphans and everyone else that the Question Marks were moving east and that no one could stop them. However, some of the West Coast brothers made it clear this would be the last club to ever patch over without a trip to California, the Question Marks' birthplace.

So it was understood and agreed: Indiana now belonged to the Question Marks. The vote was unanimous. If not for the prior evening's conflict, it would have been a harder sell, but timing is everything.

Silent Bob opened the double doors to the meeting room and peered out at the Saints, who were clustered in small groups talking. With his best poker face, he extended his right arm and pointed at them with his index finger. He turned his palm up and curled his pointing finger several times in succession. The Saints quietly followed him into the meeting.

Silent Bob returned to his seat at the table. He looked at John and then back at the Saints, now lined up in a row against the far wall. It resembled a police line-up.

"It looks like we have a problem," said John in his deep voice. He bit down hard on his cigar stub as he surveyed the men standing in the back. Some of the Saints shifted uneasily. John looked back over at Bob. "You're the one who brought them around. I think they should hear it from you."

Bob spoke up. "I'm not sure the best way to put this. John is right: We got a problem." He paused to allow the tension to build. "We might not have enough Question Mark cuts for your mob."

The room erupted in laughter and mock combat.

The confident Silent Bob broke out the new denim vests he'd had made, sporting all the patches that identified the newest members. As the new Question Marks were swarmed by their older brothers, the Saints from Hell became part of the past. The patch that had served them well would now only be seen memorialized on the walls of former members.

Spirits were high as the large group assembled for the ride into Sturgis.

Jack was happy John had kept the feelings he expressed to Robert and him in Grand Junction between them. John was a good leader, and knew that now was not the time; there had been enough distractions.

John hand-picked the riders who would head the pack. The hundred or so bikes would be a long procession, and they wanted members who would rise to the occasion up in front.

Old Man John and Dick Woods led the pack. Behind them rode Silent Bob, Jack, Robert, and an army of Question Marks, many itching for a confrontation. while Jack's attitude was to avoid conflict at almost any cost, John knew he could count on him if the Orphans were waiting. It was maybe the right balance in a showdown.

The members were ready. Screwdrivers, wrenches, and ball-peen hammers hung from their wrists on short rawhide straps. Jack had attached his KA-BAR knife, inserted into a sheath attached above the pocket on his vest.

As always, Robert had dressed to impress. His thinking was if it was a battle, he was going down in style if that was his fate. He had altered his short black whip by braiding in a large ball bearing at the end. It had more than enough power to deliver a knockout blow to anyone unfortunate to be on the receiving end. He sported a black leather gauntlet on each forearm, stamped with the Question Mark logo. His shoulder-length hair was held back by a black bandana with a logo that was the exact match to the gauntlets.

The ride was fast and furious to Main Street, as the Question Marks invaded the streets of Sturgis. If any Orphans were present, they disappeared into the fabric of the town, not to be seen again at that year's Black Hills event.

As the Marks immersed themselves in the event, their entrance was greeted with approval. All eyes were on Robert as he strolled down the middle of Main Street in search of his prey. The following year in Sturgis, the hot items at the vendors' booths would be gauntlets, headbands, and leather hand whips, all thanks to Robert's attire.

Any thoughts the Orphans still entertained about entering the streets of Sturgis all but vanished. The Question Marks now lined both sides of Main Street and, along with the police, shared dominance of the town. Law enforcement broke into a handful of two-man teams in an effort to regain at least an appearance of control.

Walking down Main Street, Robert had five officers following him. One in the group sported a black T-shirt, identical in design to the BET jackets. All observers agreed that Robert's cavalier lone walk was the performance of the day, cops or no cops.

John and Jack mingled around the entrance of Gunner's, while the old man puffed on his cigar. It soon turned into a reception line of sorts, with Question Marks, small clubs, independents, and some tourists wanting a handshake and a quick picture.

Across the street on the second floor of a nondescript building, a high-speed camera was mounted on a tripod, manned by a professional photographer used by local police. Sergeant Sherman, Bob Ingram, Bill Bradley, and ATF agent Scott waited in the room. All but Scott and the photographer were seated at a table drinking coffee and exchanging war stories. Scott was at the window next to the tripod, but not close enough to reveal his position. He had yet to say a word.

"Him!" Scott told the photog. "I want continuous close-frame photos of all three." Someone he had been waiting for had approached the old man and Jack in front of Gunner's bar.

"You should just get a movie camera if you need them that close in sequence," replied the photographer curtly.

Oblivious to the sarcasm, Scott looked the photographer in the eyes. "Good idea," he said in a low voice. "I want one here by tonight."

Visibly taken aback, the photographer said he would do his best.

Scott didn't have to ask Bradley to move to the window; they had worked as a team more than once and could read each other's body language. A man in his early thirties talked casually to Old Man John and Jack. This man, a man from the East, was wearing a new Question Marks vest.

The sight of the two men salivating as they peered out the window made it obvious to Sherman that something big had just happened. So although he had no idea what he was looking for, he joined them at the window. He said nothing but made his presence known.

By late afternoon, both a still and a movie camera were positioned in the window. Both provided a tremendous vision of the street, but the verbal exchange was a mystery. If they'd had audio, they would have captured what started as introductions, turning to opinions, which Jack saw as bragging from an upstart.

Something didn't sit well with Jack about this new member from the East. He didn't like Archie's looks or personality. Archie wanted to ride into Rapid City and finish what Dave and Brownie had started less than twenty-four hours earlier. John took his cigar and flicked off the ash, a habit he developed over the years when he was at a loss for words.

With a glance toward Jack, John smirked at Archie and asked, "And then what? We ride off into the sunset?" John put the cigar back in his mouth. "Kids..."

Jack glared at Archie, and almost lost his composure. He did not like this guy and thought he should end this now, but Archie remained on-topic and pivoted his approach. "Yeah, I get it. Anyways, what the hell happened here the other night?" His question was really addressed to Jack since John was now talking to a small group of local club members known as the Ghost Riders.

"I really don't know," Jack told him. "I wasn't here."

Jack excused himself and disappeared into Gunner's, he didn't like the feeling this man—this new brother—had left him with. Archie was about five-nine, medium build, but soft looking. His blond hair had a slight curl to it, and perhaps that's why it was cropped short. Many club brothers embraced his loud, boisterous behavior, and his rise in the ranks of the Question Marks was second only to Jack's. The relationship between Jack and Archie was a mixture of oil and water right from the start.

Jack's dislike of Archie was so great, he felt like he would have no problem offing the guy. But the haunting memories of the night in the whorehouse kept him from acting on his emotions. Also, as much as Jack resisted, he recognized that the intoxicating mixture of power, money, and fame were becoming a weakness. He could only hope he had the strength to resist that unholy trinity and prove to himself that his anger against Archie was not just a projection of his own shortcomings.

Jack found Dick Woods, Silent Bob, and Smokey in the back of Gunner's, sharing a table with a pitcher of beer. They were working on a revolving shift of members to remain on the streets of Sturgis for the last few days of the event. This would keep any patch-wearing Orphans off the streets, at least for this year.

The daily afternoon thunderstorm had just broken and the four of them, joined by Old Man John, walked through the wet streets of Sturgis. They were amazed at the crowd of fast-buck vendors pushing merchandise on the masses. One booth caught the attention of the small group. Various painted scenes of real and imagined outlaw bike scenes were displayed in frames.

One, in particular, entitled "Tecate Run," stood out. It was a picture of a small town burning in the distance as a pack of outlaws rumbled out of the town on their bikes. "See what I'm talking about," said Smokey, repeating his favorite saying.

"Yeah," agreed Silent Bob. "That's bullshit—we only burned one street."

"Yeah," said Dick Woods, deadpan, "but that town was only that one street!" They all joined in the laughter as they moved on.

As the Black Hills Rally came to an end, the Question Marks said their goodbyes and left in small packs heading east and west. In smaller groups, they could move faster with less attention from law enforcement. The cops always had less interest when outlaw riders were returning home.

The Question Marks heading east were concerned about contact with the Orphans, but Big Jim's decision to hold his club back in Rapid City for a few days effectively ensured that their paths would not cross.

Jimbo wasn't worried about a confrontation that would jeopardize the safety of fellow Orphans. His decision was based on the fact that confrontation was bad for business. As far as Jimbo and other influential Orphans were concerned, money was as important as a brotherhood. Without the money, there was no Orphan brotherhood.

They were ahead of their time. Eventually, huge legal fees would present a challenge to all outlaw bike clubs.

The BET unit, along with their federal associates, felt the time and money spent in Sturgis would prove productive in the near future. Ingram, Bradley, and Agent Scott informed Sherman and the BET members that they would see them in California in the coming weeks. They would forward the necessary information directly to Sergeant Sherman prior to their arrival in Ventura, and expected everything to be in order when they got there. With that, they said their goodbyes.

Jack and Robert packed their bikes for home, but for the first day would only go as far as Cody, Wyoming. Jack had been waiting for this trip since he had come back stateside, as had his old military buddy, Keith, who was awaiting his arrival.

First, though, Jack and Robert needed to resolve the issue of Peggy, the dancer Robert had brought from Grand Junction. As promised, she had been no trouble. Robert wasn't ready to put her on a bus home.

She stood out, with stylish short black hair and a stunningly beautiful face. She was tall and slender, and her muscles were defined from years spent dancing. In fact, she'd been one of the few girls that night who could actually dance. Not long after they had first started talking, Robert realized she could accomplish anything she put her mind too. She was from Georgia, had attended private schools and had an accent he couldn't get enough of. It was likely she came from money.

Robert had never felt this way about a woman before. He saw her as his equal. But Jack sensed that Robert was uncomfortable imposing on Jack. Jack decided to relieve his club brother's stress with a simple gesture of goodwill. He handed Robert two pairs of earplugs for the day's ride.

"You and Peggy will need these when we go through the Big Horn Mountains; the pipes really echo off those cliffs."

Robert embraced Jack, thanking him. As Jack mounted his bike, he watched Robert helping Peggy with her earplugs, and he tried to push thoughts of the Vietnamese girl whose life he had extinguished out of his head.

Cody was one day's ride from Bella Fourche. The three of them traveled west until they came to Wyoming State Route 14, which took them over the Big Horn Mountains, one of God's gifts to man. Then they made their descent into the town named after Buffalo Bill Cody.

Keith was expecting them. He made sure he was on duty so he could stop and see his old friend as soon as Jack pulled into town. Jack, Robert, and Peggy were enjoying a pancake dinner at Pappy's House of Pancakes when Keith arrived.

"Hey, Marine!" Keith called out from across the restaurant. Jack jumped up to greet his old friend. They shook hands, and the handshake turned into an embrace. Jack looked Keith over and then, with a smile, said, "Nice uniform."

Keith looked Jack over and said, "You have a hell of a uniform yourself."

Jack introduced Keith to Robert and Peggy, giving Keith the title of "the second best Marine Scout Sniper in the world."

"I'm not going to ask who's the best," joked Robert.

Peggy gave her usual pleasant smile.

They all talked for a bit, then Robert and Peggy left to check out the town. They told Jack they'd wait for him later at the bar across the street.

Jack and Keith sat quietly once they were alone at the table. For a while, they just looked at each other.

Jack finally broke the silence. "I wasn't sure we were going to make it home."

Keith answered in a soft voice. "I'm not sure we are home sometimes."

"It's better than it was, right?" Jack said.

"Jesus Christ, listen to us," Keith said. "Hey, what do you want to do while you're here? Your call."

"It's your town—you tell me."

"Let's go shooting at the Marine Reserve Unit range. And you have to see the Cody museum, best gun collection in the World."

Keith offered up his house as a place to stay. But after all, he had been through with law enforcement since his return from the military, Jack decided against it. He wasn't sure he would even share this part of his life with his old friend. Only time would tell if they were still that close.

They spent the next few days at the Marine Reserve rifle range, and both Jack and Keith were surprised at Robert's natural ability with a weapon. Peggy helped police the brass and took some shots. She continued to add a level of class that only the right woman can bring to the table. Men were naturally drawn to her, but she only had eyes for Robert.

Jack was happy he had taken the time to visit his friend. Although they now wore different uniforms, their bond still held tight.

They said their goodbyes, and Keith promised to stop in to see Jack when he came to Los Angeles for SWAT training.

The bikes could still be heard heading out of town when the police chief approached Keith. "I hope you know what you're doing." It was a statement, not a question, about the company he was keeping.

"Well, I don't know about me, Chief," replied Keith cryptically, "but they seem to know what they want."

The ride through Yellowstone Park was a much-needed distraction. Jack, Robert, and Peggy took the whole day to get to Jackson Hole. For a brief period, they seemed like any other tourists on vacation.

They traveled further west toward home, and as the bikes rumbled past car after car of vacationing families, Jack's imagination put him in those cars. He wondered who really had the better life. He had second thoughts from time to time but knew he had now reached the point of no return. And when Jack returned home, he would slip deeper and deeper into this life he had chosen.

By the time Jack and Robert pulled into the ranch, John was already back at work loading up cars onto haulers for one of the studios. Dick was using a come-along to secure the vehicles in place. Brownie was sitting on an old couch shaded by a tree branch. Hanging from the tree were several sticky fly strips covered with dead and dying flies. Amber, Brownie's new love interest, was using a large, handheld fan to circulate air and keep the flies from landing on Brownie. Amber and Brownie each wore Brownie's new business venture: fly-strip hatbands. Brilliant as Brownie felt the idea was, it would never catch on. Jack laughed to himself and told Robert he could see him sporting one next year in Sturgis.

Robert just smiled.

Things weren't much different than when they left, but it was good to be back home. They all shared stories of their trips home.

Robert walked Peggy around the ranch, and then they took off to his place. Jack had considered getting a room for the night because he hadn't managed to nail down a place to stay since the fire, but he found the clubhouse couch too inviting.

While Jack slept, Sergeant Sherman was very much awake. His BET station had been alive with activity long before the sun had come up.

Sherman had plans.

Agent Scott was briefing him, along with his BET team members and teams of various local patrol units that would assist in the morning's work: the serving of a search warrant on the ranch, described in detail and identified as "Question Marks National Headquarters."

Several other locations would also be receiving early morning visits. They were described as "personal dwellings of members and/or safe houses," which could be hiding the articles described in the sealed affidavit supporting the search warrants.

Agent Scott, still identified only by the first name, had taken command of the operation because he was the contact for a confidential informant. The CI, as the contact was referred to, had provided the information that was making the morning's events possible.

Bill Bradley sat in the back of the briefing room, and Scott intentionally didn't introduce him. Sherman, Scott, and Bradley all realized this was an exercise in futility. The evidentiary items of clothing and weapons from the fight in Gunner's Bar were long gone, and they knew it. They didn't have a positive identification of the participants in the altercation either. In the sworn affidavit, the CI identified them only as "Ventura County Question Marks."

The BET vehicles, along with the black-and-white squad cars, spread out like tentacles on an octopus encompassing their prey. Scott and Bradley took it to another level by donning ski masks to protect their identities. The energy was high as they swarmed the ranch.

As the door came down, Jack jumped to his feet. Agent Scott was the second one through the door behind Cory. If not for Cory's identifying BET jacket, Jack would have emptied his .45 into Scotts hooded form. Instead, he dropped the gun onto the couch.

John stumbled out of the bedroom with an unlit cigar in his mouth and a grin on his weathered face. "Good morning, gentlemen."

Similar doors were being shattered open all over Ventura County. The raid turned out to be a bust as far as tangible evidence was concerned, evidence that was supposed to cinch the prosecution of outlaws for something that had happened halfway across the country.

Bradley finally ran across something in the main house of the Hayward ranch. It was something he could spin to the media to make the Question Marks name a menace.

Years later, it would remain a matter of debate if the house, being a separate dwelling, should have ever been entered or was intended to be searched when the judge signed the warrant. John explained that he had no access to the main house. Sherman and the still-hooded Scott and Bradley huddled briefly, reentered the house, and started the tedious task of removing Mr. Hayward's large personal gun collection. It took hours to register the weapons' serial numbers so that a proper receipt and record could be left on the table. Mr. Hayward had legally purchased all the guns. And he was a powerful man with influential friends—and attorneys.

Cory walked Old Man John and Jack over to the sofa under the tree, where he moved their cuffs from the back to the front.

"What the hell are you doing with Sherman?" Jack asked Cory. Jack snarled at him. "This isn't an investigation, it's a witch hunt, and you know it."

John nodded, backing Jack up. "And that's the last we have to say to you."

Cory looked at the ground and answered softly, "I go where the investigation takes me."

CHAPTER FIFTEEN

The next morning, the headlines in two local papers and the largest Los Angeles paper read: "Over 200 Guns and Drugs Netted in Outlaw Biker Round-up. Is This the End of the Question Marks Motorcycle Gang?" Over the years, this would turn out to be the best headline BET and Sherman would ever get from the Question Marks.

The chief, wanting to justify the additional spending on the BET unit, set up a press conference on the steps of the courthouse for noon. Various people congratulated Sherman as he and the chief walked through the courtroom halls.

The chief stood at the podium and greeted the crowd, thanking them for taking the time to see the fruits of BET's not only hard but dangerous work. "Our county, our city," he went on to explain, nodding in acknowledgment to the City of Ventura's mayor, "was not only part of the ground floor of this fight against this new cancer attacking the very fiber that holds our country together, but they were leading the fight.

"Over the last few weeks, this Biker Enforcement Team has chased the Question Marks gang halfway across the country and back, with the help of specially trained federal agents. I want to personally thank them, and introduce Sergeant Sherman and his BET Unit, and then we will take some questions."

After the introductions, the chief directed everyone's attention to the table in front of the podium where the gun collection is taken from Mr. Hayward ranch home—some of them valuable antiques—were displayed along with other assorted articles. An older Question Marks three-piece patch was strategically placed on the table so the community could become familiar with this symbol of evil.

The small group of reporters began firing questions at the chief.

"How many of these weapons are illegal?"

"How many arrests?"

"How many members live in our community?"

Jack stood at the rear of the crowd, sporting a baseball hat pulled low and dark glasses, watching the carnival-like show. One reporter peaked his interest.

A female reporter quietly waited for the questions to subside, then asked a series of her own. The first, addressed to the chief, was: "What are the Question Marks doing with what appear to be antique guns?"

To which the chief replied, "I am not at liberty to say."

"Okay, why were there no arrests? Can we talk about that?"

The chief raised his hand in an authoritarian posture to stifle this young women reporter. In a condescending manner, he replied,

"This is an ongoing investigation, and all your questions will be addressed in time."

The reporter yelled out one final question: "Then what is the purpose of today's press conference?"

The chief ignored her and thanked everyone for attending. In closing, he once again thanked Sherman and BET. With that, the press conference came to an abrupt end.

As the female reporter walked by Jack, scribbling on her notepad, he shot her an offhand comment. "Nice dog-and-pony show, huh?"

The reporter stopped and turned the page in her book. "How do you see this?" she asked.

Jack had a feeling he hadn't felt in a long time.

"Well, I have a vested interest in all this."

She looked up at Jack with a puzzled expression as she continued to take notes. "Can I get your name?"

"Jack Crest."

"And what's your interest? A concerned citizen?"

"A little more than that, Miss."

She looked into his eyes, and Jack looked down and saw that her ring finger was bare.

"What would that be, Jack Crest," she asked in a low voice.

"I'm a member of the Question Marks."

Surprised, but obviously intrigued, she extended her hand.

"Nikki Swift, L.A. Times."

As they shook, she asked if she could buy him a cup of coffee.

Nikki was an up-and-coming player in the news world and had received acclaim for her honest, hard-hitting reporting. Although she was older than Jack, he was instantly attracted to her.

She was about the same height as he was, with a pretty face, and dark hair cut in a short pixie style. She wore black-framed glasses and hip clothes that gave her the look of an intellectual bohemian. As a graduate of Berkeley's School of Journalism, she had been connected to the whole Bay Area counterculture.

The two ended up talking for hours.

The conversation finally came to a close when Nikki headed back to the newspaper to work on her story for the Sunday edition, and Jack made his way back out to the ranch. He needed to talk to the old man. He had just done something he had never been done before, given an interview to a newspaper reporter. He wasn't sure how it was going to fly. It wasn't against the rules, but instinctively he knew it would be received with mixed reviews.

When Jack arrived, John had just finished meeting with Mr. Hayward and his lawyer. Hayward had regretfully told John that he was sorry, but that he had been advised by his attorney to sell the property. It had become clear that it was time for Mr. Hayward to separate himself from the Question Marks.

Hayward informed John that there was some positive news in all this. The motion picture prop and car rental business would continue with John as it had before all this unfortunate trouble. The business would relocate to two large airplane hangars near the Santa Paula Airport, which the Hayward estate had just purchased. But with the exception of Old Man John and Dick Woods, it would be absent of any Question Marks. That prohibition would ensure the return of the valuable antique gun collection. The powers that be had reached the agreement, sealed with a handshake.

John and Jack exchanged their information and set up the last meeting of the Question Marks Motorcycle Club to be held at the Somis ranch, the club's birthplace. It was indeed the end of an era.

Nikki's newspaper article came out, and it was a scathing account of the BET team and their actions. In an attempt to reconstruct their client's image, Mr. Hayward's attorneys had also attacked the BET team and their actions but had also made it clear that their client had no knowledge of the transition the ranch had been going through. Their statements had just as much duplicity as the chief's press conference.

The one statement that rang true was that the ranch would soon be vacant. Word had now circulated that events were happening and that there was no way to stop them. Old Man John came forward to the charter about what he had told Jack and Robert in Grand Junction and had wanted to share with the club on a national level in Bella Fourche.

To his surprise, he didn't receive the resistance he had anticipated. That hurt a little. However, it helped him come to terms with the fact that he had done the right thing. His time had come and gone.

He asked Jack, as vice president, to take charge. The first

thing Jack asked for was a vote of confidence to act as temporary president. It was unanimous, and he promised elections within the month.

As the diplomat he was becoming, Jack explained to the charter why he'd chosen to do the interview and hoped they understood it needed to be addressed on the spot. There was some resistance, but in the end, there weren't any strong objections.

After that, a piece of paper was passed around the room warning the members that BET had been in the meeting room for hours and the security of the location could have been compromised. Jack has also written the date, time, and location of the next meeting. It was set up at a campground just up the coast from Ventura. Members would camp overnight, so the site wouldn't appear to be being used as a meeting location. Times had changed, and all the Question Marks were coming to terms with it.

Nikki's article was the talk of the county. Although it slanted toward the Question Marks, it divided readers down the center. The way the article was written tapped into the political views of whoever read it, which in turn polarized an already divided community. The readers who felt the country's ideals had been compromised, and who wanted to return to times when it was unpatriotic to question authority, cheered BET on.

On the other side of the issue, the Question Marks represented freedom to many, and everything the forefathers fought for. The editor told Nikki he now expected a series of stories. He had no opinion on the subject; his agenda was selling newspapers. But Nikki had her own agenda. She didn't want to compromise her interest in this mysterious man, Jack Crest.

Leading is never easy. Although Jack had known his call to arms would come soon, he never imagined it would be under such chaotic circumstances. He had a big task ahead of him and felt he needed to seize power fast and with a clear vision if he was going to be an effective leader.

His first focus was on the Question Marks having been uprooted. As the new patriarch, his first order of business was to find somewhere to plant their flag. Jack had been in the market for a house. But now that the tenure at the ranch was over, he started looking for the place that would accommodate not only him but also serve as a clubhouse.

After the raids, he went to the man he had always turned to for things of this nature, his Uncle Pete. Jack needed to find out what this BET team was all about. Pete didn't know much but was able to find out they were housed at the old base not far from the Hayward ranch. Though obviously, if they had put the effort to follow the Marks to Sturgis, the distance would not deter them.

After some consideration, Jack felt that downtown Ventura would serve them well. The City of Ventura had its own police force and didn't like the sheriffs pushing too hard in their jurisdiction. The fact that the Ventura Police did not show up for the BET press conference showed that they had little or no interest in BET operations or the Question Marks. It wouldn't stop BET, but Jack hoped it would make things a little harder for Sherman's crew.

Jack was also hoping that having two different agencies take an interest in the club would create a less secure line of communication between departments.

He found a warehouse in a heavy industrial area, of mixed

commercial and residential zoning. This allowed twenty-four hour a day activity as well as Jack's own occupancy as a resident. Jack had his attorney negotiate for the building and made sure the payments were drawn from the interest of his estate, rather than the principal. He had begun to embrace his financial independence and to protect it.

Jack knew that for the club to make a decision as important as this one could take weeks. So like many things he did—and at times took criticism for—he shot from the hip in an effort to move things forward. He had a small sticker on his bike that read "No guts, no glory." He lived by the motto.

When the members arrived for the next meeting, scheduled as the "camp out," they were given a map and told to follow the directions to a new location. There they found Jack milling around what would become the new home of the club.

John was a very happy man. Jack's gesture helped take the weight of guilt off his shoulders. Although the chain of events that ousted the club from the Hayward ranch had nothing directly to do with John, he still carried the burden in his heart.

The older members gave Jack the support he needed. Before the evening ended, Jack knew he'd made the right choice to get the charter grounded as soon as possible. Jack's attorney did the negotiating and represented him in the transaction. The property was bought under the name QMMC, Ltd. This would protect individual parties from BET's misrepresentation of facts as they did in the recent raids.

Jack's "right choice" was a two-story building at the extreme west end of the town, less than a mile from the beach. It happened to be the roughest part of town as well.

There was a bread and pastry company located across the street, and the drivers had been the target of a rash of armed robberies. The company also fell victim to fuel siphoning and general theft.

Given the BET's press conference, the drivers petitioned the main office to move the company's warehouse. The general manager, a guy named Chuck, was told to figure something out or they'd replace him with someone who could.

The first thing the Question Marks did after moving in was mount floodlights that lit up the area as if it were daylight. It didn't take long for the first confrontation.

A small group of members had partied into the early morning hours, and although the music was blaring, you could hear the sounds of metal cans banging in the night air.

Gas thieves had been sucking the trucks dry of fuel for months, so the drivers had been instructed to return to the loading docks with as little gas in their tanks as possible. What they saved in stolen fuel was lost in man hours. The new procedure had been concocted by a college graduate who had never worked a day in the field in his short privileged life but was now the order of the day.

Jack looked out the grated steel door and saw a group of gas thieves. He calmly informed Robert and Dave that he would be telling them to leave.

He crossed the street, coolly approaching the group. He told them to move on in a pleasant voice. Jack didn't say that they shouldn't steal gas. He just informed them not to do it on that street anymore. The thieves replied that it would be best for him to mind his own business, and move on.

It wasn't a suggestion that Jack exactly embraced.

He kicked over one of the cans, and the biggest of the four men jumped to confront Jack. Robert, who was now standing at the door, had never seen Jack in a confrontation. He decided to hang back in the shadows for a bit.

As the tallest gas thief attempted to shove Jack's shoulders, Jack made a half fist and extended his right thumb. His fist hit the man on the adams apple, and his thumb went deep into the soft part of the thief's neck. The thief panicked as he fought to breathe. Seeing their leader in great distress, the others began to fight out of fear.

Robert closed the short distance to the trucks and joined Jack in dispatching the remaining thieves. The thieves' car was parked down the street. Inside was a large, vicious-looking mix of a dog. In their panic, someone whistled for the dog—General—to assist them. The animal launched through the back window that had been rolled down just enough to allow him to come to their aid if needed him.

And come he did.

General was quickly closing the space between the car and his master when a second Question Mark emerged from the shadows of the door. Gypsy from Venice had armed himself with the High Standard Pump Riot Shotgun that was kept ready by the door of the clubhouse. Gypsy tracked General's line and then aimed just a bit ahead of him and fired. General never knew what hit him; he tumbled dead in the street. The thieves broke and ran, leaving the gas cans, siphon hoses, their car, and General's body behind. Within seconds, the car had all its windows broken, all its tires slashed and was ransacked. Darcie was attempting to burn it to the ground when Jack called everyone into the clubhouse.

The first Ventura Police patrol car soon pulled up. Jack emerged from the clubhouse and stood by the door. The officer walked over to General, perhaps in an effort to see if the animal was suffering.

"Too bad, nice-looking dog," he commented to Jack.

He walked over to the abandoned gas cans and siphon hose between two of the trucks. Then he turned his attention to the car that now appeared to have been abandoned there for months.

The first thing the officer asked was, "How do you like the neighborhood?"

"Well it's a little different than the ranch," Jack replied. "We aren't used to newborns."

"So it appears," the officer replied. "Can I get your name?"

The cop's name was officer Cubes. Cubes had an interesting background: a Vietnam Green Beret Major who helped pick up where the French left off. Rumors in the department ran wild about his exploits while he was in the country. He'd remained a street officer for over three decades and never petitioned the department for a single promotion. Jack wasn't sure if he liked him, but he took him seriously and respected him for the next twenty-five years as a VPD Officer.

"My name is Jack Crest."

Jack wasn't sure if he should extend his hand, due to the

circumstance of the officer's visit. He glanced at the sticker on his bike—No guts, no glory—and thought, What the hell? As they were shaking hands, the next unit pulled up, and the officer exited his car. Cubes said to the officer, who was a corporal, "Paul, can you get Jack's ID?"

It was easy to see who was in charge. Jack extended his ID to the newly arrived officer, who took it with his left hand and extended his right to Jack. As they shook hands, the corporal introduced himself as Paul.

Cubes and Paul made their way over to the lifeless but once valiant dog. They talked just out of range of Jack. But what Jack couldn't hear, he could see as Cubes pointed his large Maglite up the street.

In the center of the light's beam were three figures handcuffed in a daisy-like chain to the spotlight of the black-and-white patrol car. The tallest was cuffed to the car, then in order of their height came the next, with the shortest on the end of the human chain. It was a comical sight. Over the years, Jack always wanted to ask Cubes if the order of height had any significance, but he never did.

Chained together were the bullies of the west end of town, the Jones brothers. The three brothers, along with their cousins and friends, had terrorized the streets for years. What made this night different than any other was that the three brothers did something they had never done before; they turned to the police for help. Whether out of fear or desperation, it didn't matter. Trying to find an honorable exit from this mess they had gotten themselves into with the Question Marks, they broke the golden rule of the street and called the cops.

But the story they told was not only full of lies, but it was also filled with holes that the VPD saw right through. They told Cubes that they were walking down the street when they came upon several Question Marks stealing gas from the trucks. After a savage beating and the murder of their dog, they ran for their lives. They could not explain their gas-soaked clothes and hands, or why—since they were walking—their car was parked near the trucks targeted for the gas theft.

Cubes and Officer Paul talked things over then returned to Jack to get his side of the story. Of course, Jack told them that he didn't know what had happened. Then, in an effort to set the standards for future police contact, he told them that even if he were aware of any information, he couldn't share it with them.

As an afterthought, he added, "No disrespect intended."

"None was taken," replied Cubes. "I think it's important we understand each other." Cubes went on, "It looks to me like things finally caught up with the Jones brothers. We'll call tonight's events 'street justice.'"

As he smiled at Jack, Corporal Paul added, "No use clogging up the courts."

They returned Jack's ID and said goodnight. The two officers walked up to the three brothers and proceeded to remove the handcuffs. The big one looked confidently at his brothers, and said, "Goddamn right," as he rubbed blood back into his wrists.

Cubes then went on to tell them, "This is what's going on. I would bet my life those are your cans down the street. But since you stated they aren't yours, they're now mine. I'm giving you until my shift starts tomorrow to remove your car. If not, at the start of my shift, I'll have it towed. As far as your dog, I'm not going to cite you for not having him on a leash.

"I think your tenure in this town has come to an end, but that's just my opinion. Goodnight, gentlemen."

By now, the drivers had started arriving, along with animal control to remove General. Cubes gave the bread drivers the gas cans along with the information he speculated had happened, and he was pretty damn accurate.

Not long after the VPD left, there was a knock on the clubhouse door. It was the manager of the bread company, Chuck. His arms were full of pastries and bread. He introduced himself and told Jack he was the "welcome wagon" for the neighborhood. Jack invited him into the clubhouse. It began a long, friendly relationship between the drivers and the Question Marks.

It was just one of many friendships that Jack was able to cultivate over the years, friendships with people who seemed worlds apart from his lifestyle.

CHAPTER SIXTEEN

Over the next few months, the members did a lot of work on the new location. Old Man John and Dick Woods were seen less and less in the daily business of the club, but they continued to attend meetings and stay relatively close, in both proximity and support. Jack knew they were only one town away and, from time to time, went to them for counsel.

The new site was an oversized commercial lot. The members converted a large shed in the corner into a workshop for the bikes. The first floor of the clubhouse was used to entertain out-of-town members and guests. It had a handmade resin-top bar with broken knife blades and brass from fired bullets encased in the resin. It made a powerful aesthetic statement.

The walls were covered with Question Mark regalia and pictures of current and fallen members. A prison cell door hung on one wall, a prop from Mr. Hayward's company. The bars had been cut with a torch in a jagged fashion as if a breakout had occurred. More pictures hung behind the frame of the broken and cut bars, photos of brothers who had gone to prison. It was a rogues' gallery of members from around the country, and it was growing.

A small bandstand filled one corner of the room. It was raised a couple feet off the cement floor. Eventually, a stripper pole would be added.

They kept the cement floor so that leaking bikes wouldn't be a problem. A regulation antique pool table dominated the center of the floor, and the club imposed a twenty-five dollar fine for laying a cigarette or drink on top of the wooden bumper rail. There was a fifty-dollar fine for anything other than a ball set on the deep red felt.

The second floor had only one entrance, which was at the rear of the first floor. It was always locked unless it was occupied. It was the Ventura County Question Marks meeting room.

A very long wooden table with matching chairs sat in the middle of the room. This is the table where, as the mother charter every week, the members made choices that could affect their brothers all around the country.

Lockers lined one wall for members to store personal items or a change of clothes. On the same wall were mailboxes; any member could use the address unless they were on parole or probation. This kept nosy law enforcement personnel honest—no warrant, no entry.

That particular feature had really burned BET's ass. They had tried with no success to use the issue of the mailboxes as a means to get to the new location. It had become BET's new obsession, and they weren't making any headway.

BET had not counted on the Question Marks moving into the heart of town. From time to time, Sherman second-guessed himself, thinking that maybe they had applied too much pressure too early. When he got a call from Ingram to fly to Washington DC, it only reinforced his fear that he had played his cards too soon.

The flight was a commercial flight, paid for by the feds. Ingram told him not to wear any police—and especially BET—clothing. That worried Sherman.

He hadn't drunk in years. On that flight, with so much on his mind, he wanted a drink badly. But he had made a commitment to the chief long ago that he would stop cold after one awful night at a bar in Camarillo.

At the end of that particular evening of drinking, Sherman had pulled his gun in a fight over a woman. Not only had his gun been taken away, but he'd also been beaten within an inch of his life by a younger Old Man John. He swore vengeance in the middle of the crowded bar. If the Chief, then a street cop, hadn't shown up, no telling what may have happened. The chief straightened it all out and, so many years later, it really wasn't important. No one even remembered who the players were.

But Sherman did.

Even Old Man John had still not recognized Sherman as the man he beat up and humiliated so long ago. As a young man, Sherman lacked control and judgment. Add alcohol to his bad temper, and it was a recipe for disaster. Sherman was given a choice that night. He decided that would be the last night he put liquor to his lips. On the plane, a still-sober Sherman drifted off to sleep wondering if his secret was out and that this was the reason for his trip.

His sleep was filled with abstract thoughts from that boozy night. When he woke up, he felt refreshed and chased all self-doubt out of his mind.

Sherman had actually been called to Washington for one reason: because he was the head of BET. He walked into the meeting room to find Ingram, Bradley, ATF Agent Scott, and a nondescript individual he didn't recognize seated around a conference table. The stranger wore boots, Levi's, and a wool shirt. Surveillance photos were plastered on the wall behind the man, some of which Sherman recognized as being from the most recent Sturgis rally.

As Sherman took a seat, an aura of heaviness filled the room. Its occupants all focused on the sergeant. In a serious tone, Ingram informed Sherman that this information was for his eyes and ears only.

"This is our undercover operative," Ingram announced. "You may recognize him as 'Archie,' a Question Mark from Indianapolis."

The sergeant's attention now focused on several pictures showing the front of Gunner's Bar. These photos showed Old Man John, Jack Crest, and the member of the Question Marks now sitting directly across from him.

Bradley spoke out to clarify that their target was Jack Crest, not the old man.

Ingram interjected, "Of course, we'll take down anyone in our path if the opportunity presents itself."

"If I remember correctly," Sherman finally spoke, "you told me, hands off Jack Crest."

"Well things are very fluid here in Washington and that order has changed."

"He was asked to get on board, and he refused," spat Bradley.

"So now," Ingram said, "Crest will be served up to a United States Federal Court."

For a moment the room fell silent, and then Agent Scott spoke up. "Archie and I will truck Archie's bike to Ventura. He'll contact Jack at the new clubhouse, to pay his respect to a new member and rising political star from the east. He'll then be called home. The cover story will be that a family member is being hospitalized with an illness. Archie will fly home with all the information he's gathered, and help us to obtain a search warrant for the clubhouse.

"Archie will be back in Indianapolis when the raids take place to keep him free of any suspicion. After the raid, he'll return to gather intelligence and move us forward in our investigation. Since his bike will be on the West Coast, he'll take that opportunity to visit members up and down California and gather more intel. We're confident this won't cause any suspicion."

"What if he doesn't gather enough information to get us a warrant," asked Sherman dubiously.

A cold expression washed over Bradley. "That's not going to happen. We'll get our warrant."

The flight back was much more relaxed for the sergeant. His confidence was up, and this time when he went to sleep, he had dreams of returning to Washington to receive his commendation from the Attorney General.

It was early morning in the California desert when the van transporting the bike for the undercover operation found a safe and convenient spot to stop and unload its cargo. Agent Scott could see the lights from Bill Bradley's car not far behind. He was parked by the side of the road as a backup. Scott knew it was Bradley by the purposely out-of-adjustment headlights, one pointing high and one low for easy identification.

Through his night-vision binoculars, Bradley watched the bike being pushed down the ramp. After the bike was secure, Scott and Archie quickly shoved the ramp back in and closed the rear doors. Archie took the spray bottle of dirty water from the side doors and began the task of making his bike look like he had just ridden halfway across the country. His clothes already looked like they had, and the next two hours of riding to the Ventura clubhouse would take care of his face and hair.

Archie kicked life into his bike, shook hands with Scott, and was on his way. They traveled together, the van following the bike. They intentionally had plates from two different states in case of a chance encounter.

A lot of time, money, and effort had been put into the operation, and all the participants hoped that the fruits of their labor would soon pay off. When they hit the end of California's State Route 126, Archie continued west while Scott headed east to BET headquarters.

Archie pulled up to the new Question Marks clubhouse, and Jack and Robert came out to greet him. They fixed him a place in the back of the clubhouse, which the members referred to as the bunkhouse. It was four small rooms, one of which Jack lived in full-time.

Archie was nervous but hid it well. This was a new type of operation, and he didn't have much information to fall back on other than common sense. He had read the file on Jack Crest, and he knew this man had killed with impunity. It was still early, but Jack suggested Archie get some rest. He knew it had been a long ride.

Archie took Jack's advice, but his rest was anything but peaceful. Alone with his thoughts, Archie had some truths to face. Straight up, Jack scared him. On top of that, Archie had never taken a man's life and wondered if he could rise to the occasion. Because Archie knew that in the room next to him was a trained assassin. And that he was the enemy.

CHAPTER SEVENTEEN

Scott and Bradley had what they figured would be their last public meeting of the trip at Denny's restaurant fifteen minutes east of Ventura. Jack had met Bradley back when the feds tried to "recruit" him, and although Bradley had changed his appearance, Jack's covert training had taught him to look for things beneath the surface. And Bradley's scar was hard to miss.

The feds had come too far to make any amateur mistakes. After all, lives were at risk.

The BET headquarters were close by, and Scott had planned to stop in. But Bradley had to decide if he was going to let BET know they were in California. He decided to stay mostly in the shadows. The only BET member to know Agent Scott's real purpose in California would be Sherman.

Scott's cover story was that he was attending a SWAT training school in Los Angeles. Any good cover story should be based in some truth, and this one was.

Two days before Scott and Bradley's meeting, Jack's old Marine brother Keith, left Cody, Wyoming. He was headed for the same SWAT training school in Los Angeles.

Keith planned on spending some time with Jack. After all, he'd be right there in Jack's backyard. But this visit would be a lot like that night in Vietnam so long ago—much would be changed forever.

Keith drove all day and into the night. When he could no longer stay awake, he pulled into a rest stop and curled up in the back seat. He woke up in the middle of the night and jumped back behind the wheel, continuing west to Ventura.

He pulled up in front of the clubhouse, parked, and then asked himself if this was prudent. Keith and Jack's lives were now worlds apart, and they both knew it.

The reservations both men felt were not apparent in the way they greeted each other. In fact, Bradley, who was positioned on a hill overlooking the clubhouse, saw this new arrival as a "person of interest."

Bradley took several surveillance photos and wrote down the out-of-state license plate number. He wrote in his notes that this man was definitely "more than a casual friend" and planned to pass this information on to Agent Scott to find out just who the new player was.

Bradley could only hope that Archie would understand the need to find out who this new individual was.

As the Marine buddies ate the breakfast that was waiting on the stove for them, they made small talk about the only things they had in common anymore: the Corps and guns.

When Archie awoke, he could hear laughter and men's voices. He laid still, trying to pick up what the conversation was about. He couldn't hear everything, but it was obvious they were talking about guns. A mixture of fear and adrenaline brought him to his feet and led him in the direction of the voices.

He entered the kitchen and asked Jack if there was any coffee. Jack pointed to the counter and suggested he finish up the bacon and eggs on the stove.

He introduced the two men, but it was a lean introduction at best. Jack wanted to protect Keith but protect himself as well. There were many members who would take exception to sitting across the table from a cop.

Jack's pensive attitude only fed Archie's suspicion. Keith and Jack ended their visit with Jack giving Keith a tour of the clubhouse. Archie watched their every move, then stood in the doorway sipping on his coffee in an effort to pick up any intel they might provide as they said their goodbyes.

Jack and Keith shook hands, and Keith drove off to SWAT training.

Jack watched his old friend disappear down the street. Archie joined him, trying to make small talk. Although he had seen the out-of-state plates on Keith's car, Archie made no mention of it. He commented that Keith seemed like a nice guy, and asked if he had an interest in the club. Jack responded with curt answers, explaining that he was a personal friend from the Marines.

Archie changed the conversation to the new clubhouse and how the members liked the new location. It was shallow, but it gave the men the opportunity to measure each other.

Jack decided to get to the point. "So what brings you out west?"

"I wanted to see where it all started and pay my respects."

"That's a long trip to make by yourself. Did you have any trouble?"

"No, I like traveling by myself. It makes for a fast trip."

As they talked, various members drifted in and out. Archie noticed something unusual. Anyone who entered the door to the upstairs had to use a key, and the door locked behind them. Also, only Ventura chapter members seemed to have access.

It was obvious to Archie that the members were protecting or hiding something up there.

It was the workings of a cop's mind.

He told Jack he needed to call home to check in, hoping the phone would be upstairs. But Jack directed him back to the bunkhouse, to the pay phone on the wall.

Archie made his call home to let his charter know he had arrived in Ventura safely. A member from his charter told him that his family was trying to make contact with him, and he should call them. He made the prearranged cover call, and for security reasons, any third party who happened to be listening would be convinced that Archie's aunt had suffered a heart attack and he should return home.

When he ended the call, he went back into the main part of the clubhouse and took a seat. He took on the characteristics of a man who had a lot on his mind, hoping someone would inquire if things were—or were not—alright back home. It didn't take long for a young prospect to ask. It was the opening Archie was looking for. He explained not just to the prospect, but to anyone within hearing distance that his aunt had suffered a heart attack and had been asked by his uncle to return home.

Jack was sitting at the table reading the paper. He lowered it and asked Archie if he needed anything. Still greedy for information, Archie made an error in judgment and asked Jack if they were having a meeting tonight.

Jack's protective instinct kicked in. Although there was indeed a meeting scheduled for that night, he told Archie it had been canceled, providing no further explanation.

"Well, I missed last week's meeting," Archie tried to explain, "so I really didn't want to miss another."

"I'm sure members will understand," responded Jack.

The two men both paused and stared at each other a little too long. Jack liked Archie less and less with each encounter. And he was positive the feeling was mutual.

Archie spent the rest of the morning on the phone, trying to confirm a flight home and reserving a car at the local car rental. He declined the offer of a ride to the L.A. airport, which struck Jack as odd. In addition, Archie chose to spend the night and leave the next day. So much for the emergency.

As the meeting time approached, members who could not be reached about the meeting's cancellation drifted into the clubhouse. Jack watched from the back as Archie made the rounds to the various members now milling around the main room.

Robert joined Jack at his vantage point, and they both took notice of Archie's interest in anyone who entered or exited the door to the upstairs room.

The next morning, Archie pushed his bike around back, got into the car he had rented, and headed south to the airport. He pulled his rental car into long-term parking and proceeded to secure his gun and personal effects in the trunk.

He then got back into the driver's seat, checked the time, closed his eyes, and waited.

Jack and Robert sat in silence drinking their coffee, eyeing each other. Jack spoke first. "I don't like that guy. He's not right."

"I can't argue with that," replied Robert. "But maybe it's a matter of geography."

"Come on, Robert. You and I both know there are some really good people back East," Jack sipped his coffee. "Well, maybe he's just not one of them. Or maybe we need to give him some time to get in step."

"Hey, he did show some class, riding his bike out here," noted Robert.

Jack was silent and then mumbled to Robert as much to himself, "Time will tell."

Archie had just started to drift off to sleep when a rapping on his window woke him. It was Scott and Bradley. Before they could even exchange hellos, Bradley asked, somewhat rhetorically, "Do you know who that guy was in the clubhouse with Jack?"

Still a bit foggy from the sleep, Archie replied, "A friend."

Bradley barked back, "He's a fucking cop out of Cody, Wyoming!"

"What did they talk about?" asked Scott.

"Nothing, just small talk. The Marines and guns."

"That's not nothing!" Bradley said. "Why is a cop from Cody at the Question Marks clubhouse?"

"Jack didn't introduce the guy as a cop. How the fuck 'am I supposed to know that?"

"That's why you're on the inside," Bradley shot back.

Before the conversation got past the point of civility, Agent Scott became the voice of reason, "Let's slow down. It's obvious they're up to something. Why did they both hide the fact that he's a cop? They most likely are doing an illegal weapons deal. Did they say anything that would give you that impression, and did they have any physical evidence that you saw that would support that?"

"No, not really. Nothing seemed out of place except for their protective posture of the second floor."

"What do you mean by that?" asked Scott.

"The entrance to the second floor was always secured, and only members enter and exit. One way in and one way out."

"You couldn't get up there?" questioned Bradley.

"No way and I tried all night," replied Archie.

"Did you see that cop up there at any time?"

"No, but he was in the clubhouse when I woke up."

"When you woke up? Well, I am glad you got your beauty sleep," mumbled Bradley. This really burned Archie but let it pass.

Agent Scott spoke up. "I want in that building by the first of the week."

"I really didn't see anything that would give us probable cause for a warrant. You want me to swear to something that's not in there? That's not smart."

"I'll get you in there," said Bradley. "You just plan on being back from seeing your aunt by the end of the week."

Agent Scott knew not to ask Bradley how he would get the warrant but had no doubt he would get them into the clubhouse.

Not long after Jack and Robert went their separate ways for the day, Jack rode out to see Old Man John. After they had greeted each other, John poured them both a cup of coffee, and they sat and made small talk. But after a few minutes, the old man asked Jack what was on his mind.

"I think we have a problem," Jack told him, looking over his coffee cup and into John's eyes.

"What kind of problem would that be?"

"That fucking Archie is no good."

John looked into Jack's eyes and said, "That's a hell of a way to talk about a brother. Have you thought that maybe you just don't like him?"

"Well, I'll admit John, on top of this bad feeling I have about him, I don't like him."

"Aside from your feeling, what has he done that gives you the right to attack his character? You know, Jack, you don't have to like him, but that patch on his back should warrant your respect."

"It's just a feeling I have, and I can't explain it. He's fucking cancer if you ask me."

"Jack, I think you're looking for someone to tell you what you want to do is okay. I'm not going to tell you what to do or not to do, but you need to think this out very carefully. What direction do you want to take the club? Think about it real hard, my young brother."

It was close to midnight when Bill Bradley came down from his observation post overlooking the clubhouse. No one had come or gone for several hours. The bars would be closing soon, which could bring some activity. He decided now was the time to make his move. He made one pass by the front door, which was swung wide open. He parked around the corner and turned off the lights, but left the motor running. The night's ocean fog was starting to drift in, which helped him hide against the fence line as he approached the open door. He pulled the pin on the hand grenade and tossed it into the main room. He was gone as fast as he arrived, a hundred percent committed to his act.

When the spoon hit the cement floor, it broke the silence. Dave was standing in the back of the room, and the sound of tin hitting another metal object caught his attention. He looked in the direction of the noise. What he saw was a dull green ball-like object skidding across the floor. For a brief moment, he chuckled to himself, "Why would anyone throw a trailer hitch into the clubhouse?"

But then the blast ripped through the main room.

The force of the explosion turned a steel work chair into what looked like a work of twisted modern art. The fragments of notched wire and ball bearings, along with the case itself, sprayed the surrounding area and Dave's body. The concussion was so forceful in the confined area that it blew the air out of the tires of the two bikes parked inside.

Jack ran out of his room. Through the smoke, he could see Dave, still on his feet but staggering. He had seen this before and immediately recognized that Dave was in shock. His first act was to secure the front door, then try to make Dave as comfortable as possible. He could already hear the sirens of the emergency vehicles of in the distance.

Bradley was back at his observation point, watching as things developed. He'd thought he saw the image of a body just before he pulled the pin, but he wasn't sure. At least that's what he continued to tell himself. At this point in his life, it didn't really matter anymore. If his mentor could see him now, he would shake his head in disgust. The first rule Bradley was taught was never stick around to admire your work.

But he couldn't resist. He liked the rush too much.

The Ventura cops and firefighters showed up at about the same time. Jack opened the clubhouse to them and stepped aside to let the EMTs attend to Dave. Things seemed to be happening at an accelerated rate, and it soon became confusing as to who was in control. Emergency medical aid was being administered to Dave, and criminal investigations were being launched by several different agencies, all of which seemed to be on the verge of colliding.

The sheriffs had shown up, and they were trying to gain control. The VPD had no bomb squad, so the sheriff's bomb unit had been called in to secure the area and to look for additional explosive devices.

Jack was still concerned about Dave's well-being and was watching the medical personnel try to stabilize him. As Jack followed Dave to the ambulance, Jack saw them: Sergeant Sherman and his BET unit.

This raised a red flag with Jack since he knew BET generally worked Tuesday through Saturday. How did they get here so fast on a late Sunday night? It was a question that lingered with Jack.

Sherman wasted no time voicing his opinion as to what happened. "This is how we see it," bellowed the sergeant. "You were building a bomb, and it went off."

"If we were going to build a bomb," Jack fired back, "we wouldn't do it here, and Dave wouldn't be the one building it."

The two men had to be separated by the VPD, who was now acting as referees. The ranking VPD officer stated for the benefit of both men and to defuse the situation, "It looks like it was an M67 hand grenade. We found the spoon."

Agent Scott stepped out of the shadows and demanded the spoon. The VPD officer told him it was now in evidence and that he couldn't do that. As Sherman and Scott stepped away to discuss the situation, Jack casually asked the VPD Officer, "Hey, what's that guy's name again."

"He's an ATF agent out of the East Coast, not sure on the name."

Jack was overwhelmed with confusion—and that feeling that had now become more familiar to him. The yellow police tape was strung across the entire front of the clubhouse, and Jack was informed that the cops would need access to all areas for their investigation, and they hoped Jack would cooperate by unlocking any locked areas so they wouldn't have to destroy anything.

The VPD went to great lengths not to damage any more property, and Jack appreciated that. Several hours had passed before law enforcement turned control of the clubhouse back over to Jack and the Question Marks.

Robert had arrived at the clubhouse just in time to ride in the ambulance with Dave. The medics had treated Dave as best they could but were concerned about possible internal injuries.

Robert demanded that they go to the nearest and best hospital, which happened to be Saint John's Catholic Hospital. The issue of insurance was brought up several times before admitting personnel decided it would be best for everyone to work it out later.

One of the BET units had followed the ambulance to the hospital. They made an attempt to get a statement from Dave as he was wheeled into the emergency room. Emotions were running high, and Robert told them to back the fuck off. Dave just stared at them in silent contempt.

The attending doctor was a young black man who did not like the fact that BET had no regard for Dave's condition or his own authority as the treating doctor. BET had even gone as far as asking the nurse to talk to the head physician in an attempt to continue their interrogation.

As the nurse gave Dave a shot of morphine, he drifted off into a dream world. He thought about his time in prison, and about the color line that the doctor had just crossed for him.

He saw the room explode again and remembered the cell he had firebombed just before his release. Then he drifted in and out of ecstasy. This suited him just fine. He knew his brother was there and he had nothing to worry about.

Jack surveyed the clubhouse and decided to keep a photo log of the damage. Things looked much worse than they actually were. Although the bomb squad would not share any information with Jack, he had taken some demolition classes and tried to conduct his own investigation.

By chance, the grenade had detonated under the steel work chair, the one now twisted into a modern art form. The chair had redirected the explosion. The cement floor had a hole several inches deep and about a foot wide. You could see that the spray pattern was directed into the east and west walls.

Dave had been standing on the north end, which most likely saved his life. As Jack made his way to the second floor, what caught his eye was that the two pump shotguns had been removed from their racks and unloaded. And, most likely, had their numbers run for origin and ownership.

Knowing that they were legal and registered gave Jack some comfort in his anger and confusion over why this had happened and who was responsible.

It was mid-morning by the time Jack completed his survey of the clubhouse. Along with many club members, the media was starting to arrive. The word was out that there had been a bombing in downtown Ventura. Everyone was asking the same question: Why? Dave's condition was now stable, and Jack knew that he would have to go outside soon and face the reporters.

And that question.

Everyone's suspicion turned to the Orphans, and it was a reasonable conclusion. As the word spread to the East Coast, the Orphans became the only suspects that the Marks cared to talk about. Jack wasn't so sure but was having a hard time getting anyone to look at the incident with an open mind. There were too many facts, as Jack saw it, that didn't point to the Orphans.

The Marks and the Orphans had been at odds for a few years, sure, but no one had been killed. And the Orphans did not have a history o using explosives. Plus, if this was them, it would take their problem to a different new level. From what Jack knew of Jimbo, it didn't add up to escalate the conflict and bring it out west.

When Jack finally went out to meet with reporters, he saw Nikki Swift walking up the street. Jack watched her every move as she made her way to the cluster of reporters, and he purposely stalled until they made eye contact and she could hear him.

"Sorry I've kept you all waiting, and I hope I don't disappoint you, but there's not a lot I know. Law enforcement has said our club members were possibly building a bomb. That's not true, and they know it. They know that someone threw a hand grenade into the building."

"How can you be sure?"

"The Ventura PD recovered the spoon that was lying in the doorway."

The questions went on. Most of them slanted in favor of law enforcement. When Jack finally had enough, he took control, chastising the reporters for not asking about the condition of the victim.

Nikki, who had been taking notes but had asked no questions, spoke up. "How is he doing? Will he have a full recovery? When will he be released from the hospital?"

Nikki then asked the million-dollar question, "Who do you think is responsible for this?"

Jack hesitated and then looked into Nikki's eyes. "I have a list, and law enforcement is right at the top."

With that, Jack said he was done.

When things broke up, Nikki approached Jack and said, in a low voice, "You didn't call."

"Yeah, I'm sorry about that. I've been really busy."

"How bad is the damage? I'd really like to have one of the staff photographers get some pictures. Could we do that?"

"Sure, give me a call," Jack replied, handing her a club card with the Question Marks logo on it and the clubhouse phone number.

Nikki took the card and with a flirty voice said, "We really should talk."

Bill Bradley had done his part and was making the drive home. The diet pills had kicked in miles ago and would deliver him home safely to Indiana without stopping. Archie and Ingram had met at a pre-designated safe house and were waiting for Agent Scott and Sergeant Sherman's phone call. All were determined to get back into the clubhouse.

Ingram was confident he had found a way not only to get back into the clubhouse but to issue several arrest warrants, using the information provided by their trusty CI, Archie. Ingram's affidavit would remain sealed to protect their source.

Archie had identified several Question Marks who had gone upstairs where the shotguns had been found the night of the hand grenade attack. Although the two weapons were legal and the clubhouse title was in Jack's name, Ingram had found a way to get his arrest warrants. Any member who was a felon and found to be in possession of a key to the upstairs room where the shotguns hung on the wall would be guilty of constructive possession of the two weapons. The investigation and prosecution would be an ATF operation supported by the BET.

Archie provided the list, and a federal judge issued the arrest warrants. Archie identified six Question Marks who were felons who had used keys to gain entrance to the second floor, where the weapons were. The federal judge had no problem issuing a search warrant for the clubhouse but gave body warrants only for the felony members on the constructive possession charge.

Not two complete days had passed before the ATF, along with the BET team and the Ventura PD made their move. Law enforcement officers from all three agencies overran the clubhouse at dawn. In just two days, the victims had become suspects in a war of attrition being waged by the ATF and BET.

Agent Scott and Sergeant Sherman headed up the search, and any care that the Ventura Police Department had taken two days earlier no longer mattered. Their raid left things in shambles, even compared to the explosion.

Meanwhile, Cody and several other BET officers staked out

various locations throughout Ventura County in their pursuit of the felony members. If the warrants were going to hold up in a court of law, the felons needed to be in possession of the key at the time of the arrest. Cody and another BET officer went to the hospital to confiscate Dave's key, and in doing so made a tactical error. They boasted to David what they wanted and why they were there. David's keys were nowhere to be found; Robert had taken them for safe keeping. But Robert was there with David when Cody opened his mouth. Robert excused himself and called everyone he could, telling them to ditch the keys.

Word spread like wildfire. All but two members that were felons and who had been in possession of a key were now free of any evidence that could link them to control the weapons. ATF and BET got only two indictments out of the operation, for a felon in possession of a firearm.

Not only did the arrests fall short of what ATF and BET had anticipated, but the outcome was also even more disappointing for them. Because of the unique circumstance of the weapons possession, the defense attorneys asked for a court trial. The federal judge was pleased that the defendants had not taken up the court's time with a long and expensive jury trial. With no fingerprints from the defendants on the weapons, it was obvious to the judge that it was a case of extenuating circumstance.

The judge explained at sentencing that the defendants could have been in New York City at the time of their arrest, but being in possession of the key gave them constructive possession. He thanked them for their honest testimony and handed down a lenient sentence of six months federal time.

Nikki delivered the series of stories her editor had asked for and ended with coverage of the trial and sentencing. The final headline read: "BET INVESTIGATION'S BIG BLAST TURNS INTO PUFF OF SMOKE."

Nikki spun the story into how the victims of an attack had become the targets of law enforcement. The lead of the story followed the serial numbers on the hand grenade spoon.

Those numbers had been traced to a National Guard Armory in Ohio. The Orphans were listed in the story as leading suspects, according to BET. But also listed as suspects—thanks to Jack Crest—was law enforcement.

Jack's position, public and private, was that there were no Orphans in Ohio. The Orphans had no connection to the grenade, and Jack's gut told him it wasn't them.

Jack also questioned what an ATF agent from the East Coast was doing at the scene of a hand grenade attack on the West Coast? It seemed so clear to Jack, but his Ventura brothers resisted his speculation that law enforcement was responsible.

The Ventura Question Marks were turning up the heat on their own president, but it would be Marks from the East Coast that would really stoke the flames.

CHAPTER EIGHTEEN

Members from around the country were calling for a meeting, and they wanted it held where the attack had taken place—in Ventura.

Jack wouldn't find out until later that Archie had used Silent Bob to push for the meeting in Ventura. Archie had also been waging a campaign against the Orphans to anyone who would listen. He was holding them responsible for the attack on the clubhouse and for David's injuries, and he was slowly gaining support. But even more dangerous, this man who would someday betray everyone's trust was becoming popular.

Based on his Vietnam experience, Jack had abandoned his chess strategy and thought this problem should be resolved with principles from the Chinese game of Go. He had felt for some time that the common enemy of the entire bike culture was law enforcement. His position was that a united front of all one-percent bike clubs across the country would put the outlaws in a position of power.

His real dream was one country, one club. But he knew it could never be achieved if the clubs' problems with each other continued to escalate. His goal would have to be achieved with the least amount of violence possible.

He knew he was climbing a slippery slope, and if he failed, it would be a hard, fast fall.

Agent Scott had told Archie to push for a meeting in Ventura. More activity around where the attack had taken place would generate more reports. That, in turn, would generate more money to finance the long-term investigation. That's when Archie began to use Silent Bob's political influence.

The investigation had come a long way fast, and a decision now had to be made: Was it time for Archie to wear a wire?

BET and the feds had considered bugging the clubhouse but had chosen against it. While tempted to wire the meeting room, they felt the VPD could not be trusted. This was a longstanding problem with law enforcement. Nobody trusted or shared information with each other. And it always proved beneficial to the target of the investigation.

The meeting was coming up fast, and the decision was pending. If Archie had secured his reputation enough, could he wire up and not arouse suspicion with the aggressive position he would take against the Orphans?

Jack knew from talk around the clubhouse that he needed to get his facts in order. His position would not be popular. Members were calling for blood, and if Jack was going to stop, or at the very least slow down the momentum against the Orphans, he'd need to propose an alternative plan to an all-out attack.

David would be a big part of that plan.

Jack had not had a serious conversation with David since the night of the attack. He asked Robert to go with him to the hospital.

David had healed enough that it was to everyone's best interest to discharge him from the hospital. The subject of payment had come up in the last couple of days, and the administrators were determined to get their money.

When Jack and Robert arrived, David was seated in a wheelchair debating with the staff how his financial obligation would be fulfilled. Hospital administrators recognized Jack as the leader of the Question Marks from the latest round of newspaper articles. When he entered, they turned the debate his way, asking that the club take responsibility.

Robert, who had insisted that the hospital admit David, politely interrupted. "This is a Catholic hospital, based on religious faith, correct?"

Although puzzled, the administrator proudly replied, "Well, yes sir."

"Then I'm sure you will receive your payment in heaven."

With that, the Question Marks excused themselves and disappeared into the night. They all had a good laugh until they turned to the subject at hand. David told them there was not a lot of information to share. There was absolutely no warning he remembered; just the round object sliding across the floor and then an explosion.

Even while they talked, David picked at metal shavings on the surface of his face, neck, hands, and arms. Each piece of metal that worked its way to the surface of his skin was carefully placed into a small clear pill bottle he wore tethered to his neck with a piece of rawhide. David had always been hard to read before, but the explosion had taken him to another level. He would become distant and quiet and would begin to live more and more in his own world.

David's parents filed a lawsuit against the Ohio armory, the federal government, and anyone else they could think of along the way. Their position was that the defendants had lost control of the explosive device, which had endangered David's life as well as public safety. The legal world found the argument interesting, and it was gaining momentum.

Jack wanted to help, but to his and everyone else's surprise, David failed to follow through, and the suit would eventually die a slow death. For a long time, Jack was not only angry but also disappointed in David. It never occurred to Jack until years later that David may have been suffering from a form of PTSD and had tried to put the incident behind him by simply not addressing it. No one could argue that even as a young man, Jack was a good leader, but there was still much about the human condition that was a mystery to him.

Archie was confident he could wear a wire undetected at the upcoming meeting. Bill Bradley had come up with an ingenious idea. The transmitter and battery would be hidden in a plaster cast on Archie's forearm. The cover story would be that Archie went down on his other bike when he returned home to see his sick Aunt.

Archie continued to use Silent Bob's influence with the East Coast members. He had even gone so far as asking what it would take for him to transfer into Silent Bob's charter. Although flattered, Bob insisted Archie remain where he had become a member and reminded him, he needed a least a year in before he could transfer but suggested he continue to interact with the older members to get the experience a leader needed.

Archie had worked hard over the previous two years to establish his relationship with Bob, first as a Saint From Hell and now as a Question Mark. He had petitioned all of the East Coast members to travel west on the same plane to show solidarity against the attack.

But there was duplicity in his every step.

Bill Bradley sat in the rear of the plane watching Archie's theatrics, drifting from member to member as the flight headed west. It was an impressive performance.

Even though not much time had passed since the attack, the Ventura clubhouse was completely back in order. Jack made sure this happened before the meeting. He knew any damage still visible would just fuel the call for revenge.

He wasn't ready to lead the club into conflict. He was already being chased by enough souls that he had left behind in a far away land, all being led by the Vietnamese girl he'd left on the whorehouse floor.

As the meeting started, Archie climbed the stairs, finally getting into the second-floor meeting room that had been the catalyst for the entire series of events, events that had come very close to taking a Question Mark life.

Robert called the meeting to order, and Silent Bob proposed that Jack, being the host of the meeting, also chair it. Bob also called for Archie to keep order, and within minutes, the two adversaries were sitting side by side at the head of the meeting table.

Roll call went quickly, and then David said a few words at Jack's request to dispel the rumors that he had suffered brain damage. After David had finished his lean description of the events on the night of the bombing, Jack asserted that everything was being done to try and establish who was responsible for the attack.

"We all know who is responsible for this attack, Jack!" Archie broke in. "And we all know what we need to do. The East has already talked about it, and we're ready to move on it."

"The East has already decided how this will be addressed?" Jack interrupted. "So where did you have that meeting? In the back of a plane?"

Silent Bob spoke up. "We didn't have any meeting," he said. And then he asked, "Why isn't John here?"

Jack wondered that himself, but remained confident he could control the conversation even without his mentor being in the room.

"Because he didn't want to be. And he's not in charge anymore. We need to figure this out with the people who are here in this room. We're the future of this club, and we have a responsibility to all members across the country. We aren't ready to go to war over suspicions, and I hope you'll all think this through."

The energy in the room shifted to Jack's position. He assured everyone that if the Orphans were found to be responsible, he'd lead the charge.

Archie tried again to shift the room but failed. Even Silent Bob seemed content to wait.

Jack ended by saying, "Let's have the next meeting in the East, with the date open until there is some real information to share."

That seemed to satisfy the room, but what really gave Jack the edge was that the old man's absence was seen as support for Jack's ability to lead. Jack found comfort in realizing that the old man was still looking out for him after all.

As the meeting broke up, Jack stood back, sizing up Archie, whom he now liked even less. Jack had politically beaten him up and was enjoying his victory when that old nagging feeling in the back of his head hit him. He focused on Archie's cast, noticing something odd.

Jack approached Archie, who had several East and West Coast members cornered as he complained about the Question Marks being perceived as weak by the Orphans.

"You're a lucky guy," Jack interrupted curtly.

"Oh, how's that?" snapped Archie, obviously in no mood for Jack's attitude.

"Well, I'm just saying, you go down and break your forearm, and walk away without any road rash. I'd say you were a damn lucky guy."

All eyes turned toward Archie, who stood there shirtless, nothing but his vest covering him. He knew he had made an error in judgment, but he had to ride it out and not back down.

"Well," Archie said smugly, "It's better luck than you've been having here in Ventura."

Jack decided to push it a little further. He invaded Archie's space, grabbed his cast, and looked him in the eyes.

"Let me sign your cast."

Jack drew a large Question Mark and signed his name.

CHAPTER NINETEEN

Back up on "Surveillance Hill," Agent Scott was in a panic. So was Sherman. The only one who seemed composed was Bradley.

They'd heard everything.

It was not a good day for them, and now Jack confronting Archie about his cast had put Archie, and the entire operation, at risk. And it was obvious by Archie's statements in the meeting that their own operative was trying to lead the Question Marks into a conflict with the Orphans.

This wouldn't fly in a courtroom. A top defense attorney would have a field day with this type of ammunition.

On top of that, they had to make a hard choice to make, either go and try to get Archie out of that clubhouse right now or to abort the investigation. They knew if Jack wanted the cast-off, it was all over for Archie.

Each agent had his own concern. Sherman spoke first. "What will they do if they find out?" Bradley looked at him in disgust. "What do you think? Crest is a killer."

"Quiet!" Scott interrupted. "It sounds like it's okay." Archie's conversation with Jack had ended, and the feds' prize undercover asset was now wandering from member to member, socializing.

Sherman was starting to have concerns as to who really tossed the grenade into the clubhouse. But he understood that the less he knew, the better for everyone involved—most of all himself.

Jack Crest was becoming an increasingly difficult problem.

After the incident with Jack and the cast, Archie made the decision to return home with the other East Coast members. The Ventura brothers told him he could leave his bike in their shop for as long as he liked. He said he'd return when his arm was healed, to ride it home.

Setting up another trip was smart thinking by Archie—and leaving now was definitely the safest posture to take. Archie made a call to his house that was rerouted to a special number for him to leave, and also receive, messages. He kept the call short and to the point. He informed the female agent on the other end of the line that he had decided to fly back with his brothers on the midnight flight and would arrive in the morning. He added that his arm was hurting too much to ride home. She, in turn, made contact with Agent Scott through a contact number.

The unholy trinity had come off the hill when Archie left for the airport with the East Coast Question Marks. Driving back to BET headquarters, Bradley opened up the conversation by handing Scott and Sherman a large folder with one hand while steering with the other.

"Remember that 'person of interest' from Wyoming?" he asked. They both listened as they thumbed through the files. "Well, it looks like we've caught a break with this guy." Bradley's voice sounded menacing.

"How is that, Mr. Bradley?" Scott shot back.

"He's a former Marine, who served with Crest. And now he's a cop."

"You're shittin' me!" Sherman blurted.

"No. No, I'm not, Sergeant."

Suddenly, the mood in the car lightened considerably.

The days passed quickly, turning into weeks. Jack was happy to see Old Man John and Dick Woods show up for the weekly meeting; it had been a while since they had made one.

For months, Jack had had his private investigator, Glen, gather as much information as possible on the feds, the BET, and the grenade attack. Jack trusted him. Glen had done all the investigation work on Jack's parents' deaths.

The P.I. was an ex-cop who had a doctorate in criminal justice. He was about five-eight with graying black hair. He was lean, with an air of confidence in his walk, but more so when he talked. He had a gift. People liked to tell him things, and he knew how to make them feel good about it.

But Glen never came to the clubhouse and would only meet with Jack at the attorney's office. He was a man of caution.

He had learned to trust Jack, so when Jack asked him to start gathering information on the Orphans, he agreed— reluctantly and with the understanding that it was for Jack's eyes only, and

Glen would retain control of the file at all times. They agreed on a handshake, and the information stayed between the two of them.

At the weekly club meeting, Jack and Robert sat at the head of the table. The old man had refused Robert's offer to sit next to Jack. He told Robert that the spot was his now.

Jack reported the information he'd gathered over the last few months, but it fell on deaf ears. Jack was not only losing support, but members were losing confidence in him. They didn't understand how a man trained to kill would not fight. John could feel the energy in the room and ended the night by asking Jack to visit him soon.

At BET headquarters, Scott, Bradley, and Sherman sipped coffee and smoked Bradley's Turkish cigarettes. Bradley had put a call into Ingram to confirm that Bradley would fly into Cody, Wyoming, to talk to Keith's superiors, and Ingram agreed to let him make the first contact by himself. Bradley would assess the situation and bring information back so they could make a decision as to whether Keith could be used as an asset.

"Where do you see this investigation going?" asked Sherman, pensively.

Scott and Bradley remained silent for a moment. Their eyes shifted to each other and then focused on Sherman. "Wherever we decide to take it," stated Bradley, matter-of-factly.

Heading to the airport, Scott asked Bradley if he was losing confidence in Sherman. Bradley never took his hands off the wheel or his eyes off the road as he slowly answered, "He will make a hell of an escape valve if it ever comes to that."

The comment ended the discussion about the BET sergeant.

John and Dick were loading a 1940 Ford Coupe onto a car transporter when they heard the sound of straight pipes off in the distance.

The old man smiled at Dick. “I told you he would come.” Dick smiled back and said nothing. After Jack rode up and said his hellos, Dick excused himself.

“Well, you got yourself in a hell of a fix, Jack,” said the old man.

“It could be worse,” Jack said. “David could have been killed.”

“That’s one way to look at it. But no matter who did this, it has to be addressed.”

“I have to tell you, my gut says this has nothing to do with the Orphans or any other outlaws.”

“You really think it’s the cops? Come on, Jack, that’s a stretch.”

“You think so? That grenade came from the east. You can’t tell me you don’t think that prick Sherman and that ATF agent don’t know something.”

“I really don’t know what to think, but you need to do something and soon.”

Jack couldn’t help feeling a like a kid being told by his dad that he had better get his “goddamn” grades up. He tried not to take it personally, but then thought, “How else am I to take it?”

He said his goodbyes, kicked life into the only comfort he was feeling and pulled out onto Highway 126.

As the telephone poles became blurs on the side of the road, Jack spotted something. He slammed on his rear brake and skidded to a stop. It was Nikki, standing at the entrance to the Santa Paula Airport.

"Well, Jack Crest, when I heard the pipes, it made me think of you."

"In a good way?" asked Jack jokingly.

"I always think of you in a good way. Haven't I shown you that yet?"

"So what's the big story this time?"

"Strictly public interest—very boring compared to your life, Jack."

"Well, I'll let you get back to work."

"Oh, I'm done," Nikki quickly replied. "Just waiting for the photographer; he's my ride."

"I could give you a lift." Jack chuckled. "If you're not scared."

Nikki shot back, "Is that a dare?"

Jack looked into her eyes and replied, "Yes, it is."

Bill Bradley flew into Cody's local airport on a small commuter plane. It was a rough ride that brought back old memories of more exciting times.

He looked like he was just another hunter, but his prey was and had been for some time, two-legged. His first stop was a coffee shop, where he saw several patrol cars parked outside.

He knew who was in there.

Bradley entered, sat in a booth in the back, and watched Keith sitting at the counter. Bradley ordered breakfast and took one last look at Keith's file as he waited. He took his time eating, wanting Keith to leave first.

After leaving the café, Bradley took a quick survey of the town. He went to the Marine Reserve Unit and made his way to police headquarters. When he entered the station, he told the desk officer he had an appointment with the chief and took a seat. Bob Ingram had called Chief Parker to set up the meeting.

Chief Parker walked out into the lobby to welcome his guest to Cody. Parker had also been a Marine Corps field officer in Korea and was now the commanding officer of the Marine Reserve Unit.

Bradley extended his hand. "It's a pleasure to meet you, Colonel."

"Mr. Bradley, what can I do for you?"

"We'd like to know if your department would be willing to loan out one of your officers."

Without hesitation, the chief responded, "What do you want with my nephew?"

Taken aback by the chief's quick uptake on the situation, Bradley cleared his throat. "Keith could be a great asset in a major investigation that encompasses several states."

"Don't you think you should be talking to him?"

"Well, we wanted to follow protocol, and if your department is not willing to work with us, for security reasons this conversation ends here."

"I'll be honest with you, Bradley. I know a few things about you, and it's not all good."

"I have served my country proudly," Bradley asserted.

"Let's stop the bullshit. We all served our country. You can have him, but it'll be his choice. Do we understand each other?"

"Yes we do, Colonel."

Nikki jumped on the back of Jack's bike. He slammed the jockey shift into gear, and they were off. At the last minute they both had second thoughts, but it was too late. Jack gently took his left hand and put it on the cheek of Nikki's ass and pulled her into his back. Nikki pushed her breasts into his back and rested her head on his right shoulder.

Jack watched her in his mirror, thinking how perfect this felt.

It didn't take long to reach the Coast Highway and his favorite fishing spot. Jack pulled to a stop in a lookout and shut the motorcycle down. He let Nikki get off first. She asked him if he came there often.

"Not as often as I used to."

They walked down to the water.

"This is where my father taught me how to fish," he told her. "You see how the tide comes in short at that one spot? Well, that means there's a hole there. That's a good place to cast your line."

"You're a fisherman or a fisher of men?" she asked.

They both laughed.

"That sounds almost biblical," Jack replied.

"Are you a religious man, Jack?"

"Not anymore," he answered, without looking at her.

"What happened?" But Nikki already knew the answer.

He ignored her and pointed to the horizon. "Sometimes you can see the dolphins and whales on their journey."

"Speaking of journeys, how would you like to come to my old stomping grounds?"

"Where would that be?" asked Jack.

"In the Bay Area. We can visit my old friends. It'll be lots of fun. What do you say, Jack Crest?"

"Would that be a date?"

"Yes, it would," replied Nikki.

Bob Ingram was already in his D.C. office when Bradley, Scott, and Archie arrived. Ingram looked around the room. "Where is Sergeant Sherman?"

"Well, we didn't contact him in time." The truth was that Scott and Bradley were indeed losing confidence in their BET colleague.

Ingram replied dubiously. "I see."

Talking to Archie, he said, "It sounds like you had a close call with Crest." Ingram never looked up as he thumbed through a stack of papers.

"Fuck Crest," said Archie confidently. "I'll personally put the cuffs on him."

Bradley was cold. "You're getting ahead of yourself. We don't have shit on him. What you said in that meeting got us nothing. But I do have some good news for you. Remember Jack's Marine buddy, the one you met at the clubhouse?"

"Let's talk about the bad news first," Archie interrupted. "What do you mean, I got us nothing? My ass is on the line."

Ingram saw the veins in Bradley's neck start to bulge. "No one is questioning your bravado or your commitment,"

Ingram told Archie, "What Bill is talking about is that you want to get into a conflict, and our target appearing to be a peacenik. That won't work. You agree, don't you Agent Scott."

"Yes, I do. But no one thinks you did anything wrong, Archie. Just listen to Bill. You're going to enjoy this."

Jack had his bike in the workshop. He had just serviced it and was packing it for the trip up north he had planned with Nikki. He still hadn't come to a clear conclusion on the clubhouse attack himself, so he decided to take no chances.

He removed a brick from under one of the workbenches to reveal a concealed small automatic pistol. He pulled on the Velcro attached to what looked like a seam sewn on the right side of his custom seat. The foam had been cut to the outline of the gun. He pulled the slide back and chambered a bullet, set the safety, and then carefully pushed the weapon into the recess with the grip facing out and to the front. This would put it into his hand, at the ready. He smoothed out the flap and wiped the greasy prints off the seat.

Archie may not have gotten the vocal support he was looking for, but he had recruited a powerful provocateur in Gypsy, the Uzi-toting Question Mark out of Venice. Gypsy was headed to Jack's own backyard, wanting answers about the attack and what was being done.

To get under Jack's skin, Gypsy had gone straight to Old Man John demanding answers. John shot him down like a duck in the water. By the time he left the old man, Gypsy knew he had made his first mistake in his quest for West Coast dominance of the club.

"Fuck that old man," he thought, his mind and body running on speed and alcohol. "He's all played out. They're both played out!"

He raced to the clubhouse as his mind churned. Jack was out front with his bike talking to Robert when Gypsy rolled up. They said their hellos, but then Gypsy abruptly blurted out, "I came here for some answers."

"Really," said Jack, looking at Robert. "What kind of answers?"

"There are a lot of people who want to know what really happened here."

"You're crowding me, brother," said Jack.

Robert said nothing as he discretely pulled on his tight-fitting leather gloves.

Gypsy just stared at Jack and didn't give any ground.

"Listen," said Jack. "Sober up and get some sleep. I'll be back next week, and we can talk." With that, Jack rode away, leaving

Gypsy standing in the street with Robert.

Robert turned to Gypsy. "I wouldn't push any harder. Jack's got a lot on his mind."

"Well, so do I. What makes him any better than me? I'm not the only one who wants answers."

Robert watched as Jack turned the corner, and then looked to Gypsy. "Sometimes things like this never have an answer."

Jack and Nikki had been on the road a couple hours when they pulled into Paso Robles. Jack's stock flathead tanks held about four gallons, and he had made it to the Bay Area more than once with just one gas stop. But that was riding alone.

It was starting to get dark, and with Nikki on the back, he decided his next stop would be Morgan Hill. It would be their last stop before they hit their destination. Nikki had a small house in Berkeley, where she had attended school. But they would make one stop first in East San Rafael. Nikki wanted to introduce Jack to some of her friends.

Gypsy made his way into the clubhouse. He had called the day before, and Smokey was waiting for him at the bar. Robert stopped long enough to make eye contact with Smokey, then he walked to the pool table.

Gypsy had been a professional bike thief years before and, along with Smokey, had stolen more bikes in Southern California than any other bike crew. They had what they thought was a code of ethics: No custom or chopped bikes, dresses only. They worked as a team. Both would dress in black leathers, and full-face helmets. They looked like dresser riders. They would cruise around in a nondescript car until they found one or more bikes.

They'd park somewhere close but safe and inconspicuous, exit through the back seat, slide on helmets, bypass the bike's ignition switch, and they'd be gone! Once the quick dismantling was through, Gypsy and Smokey would return and casually pick up the car.

Easy money.

But what made them different was they got more bikes in daylight than at night.

They were legends.

And Gypsy was dangerous. He once caught another bike crew working his area. He let them off with a warning; he only broke the leader's hands—both of them—with a ten-pound sledgehammer, on the street curb where he caught him.

Then Gypsy moved on from bike thefts into the drug business. He got in on the bottom floor as the bike culture took over the meth business. Being a dealer gave him his first taste of power. He quickly learned he could control members politically and socially with his product. If you opposed his agenda, you would suddenly find your supply cut back.

Dealing made him good money, but nothing like what he made once he upped the ante and became a drug cook. Standing next to Smokey in the clubhouse, Gypsy pulled out his bag of crank, dipped in the point of his buck knife, and held it to Smokey's nose.

Go!

Then again to the other nostril.

Go!

Then he took care of himself.

As the crank went to work, he got right to the point with Smokey. "Why aren't you running this crew? If you were the boss, this would never have happened."

Smokey's eyes watered and his nose burned from the pure crank. Coughing, he said, "We don't know that."

"Yes, we do, goddamn it! You need to step up, Smokey. There's only one way Crest will give up that spot. There it is," whispered Gypsy. "You know what has to be done."

"And have Robert and that fucking old man on my ass?" Smokey answered. "No thanks."

"I've been talking to Archie, and the East Coast ain't going to wait much longer."

"What's that supposed to mean?"

"You figure it out, Smokey."

Robert ran the balls on the table. What they were saying, he couldn't hear, but he knew he didn't like their body language.

Jack had no idea where they were going or who these "friends" were, but Nikki was anxious for him to meet them. After a fast ride over the Golden Gate Bridge, they pulled into a very earthy looking area of custom homes. Jack planted his two feet firmly to steady the bike as Nikki jumped off. With his left leg, Jack set his kickstand and swung his right leg over his motorcycle. The cold October ride had stiffened him up, and it felt good to walk the soreness out. Nikki was smiling ear to ear as Jack asked, "What are you up to and where the hell are we?"

"My parents are having a party."

Jack laughed as he waved his finger at her. "I thought you said some friends?"

"My parents are my friends." Nikki waited for a beat, looking at her shoes. "I was worried that you wouldn't have come if I told you it was my parents." She smiled at him. "But we're going to a party, not just to meet my parents.

Nikki made the trip up every year to her parents' pre-holiday party. It was a once-a-year get-together of liberal and conservative intellectuals. Her parents were both Beat Generation bohemians. Harry, who answered to Hank, was a tall, good-looking middle-aged man with a strong natural frame. His dark, uncut hair and graying Van Dyke beard gave him the look of a poet.

Nikki's mother, Sylvia, looked like she could have been Nikki's older sister—which suited her mother just fine. Nikki's parents had made it big in concert promotion, with the early Bay Area music explosion. They enjoyed their money even as they both harbored guilt about their financial success. But it wasn't enough guilt for them to abandon their pursuit of the American Dream. They passed their progressive ideology as well as a Berkeley education onto Nikki, who liked nothing more than to hold their ideology, to the philosophical fire. Nikki had tested them for years and felt Jack's presence at the party would be a good exercise for her parents.

The older couple watched out of the plate glass front window as Nikki and Jack situated themselves after the long ride. They both observed the large Question Mark patch on Jack's back but kept their thoughts to themselves.

Nikki had mentioned to her parents that she might bring Jack. She explained that he had been a subject of a recent controversial article she had written, and also made sure copies had been available to her Bay Area friends.

No one was surprised—including her parents—when Nikki showed up at the party with Jack. Some of the guests saw him as a bit of a misunderstood modern-day outlaw, while others saw him as a revolutionary. Of course, some saw Jack as a common criminal, or maybe he had become all three. The introductions were a bit awkward, but after a couple of shots of tequila, Jack settled into the scene. His firsthand experiences in the war made him the center of the conversation. He enjoyed the political banter between the two groups that divided the party for and against the war. Emotions in the room started rising along with the voices, when Nikki interrupted the debate with an exclamation, as an old friend entered the room.

"Well I know where he stands on this discussion," laughed Nikki. It was Stanley August Owsley famous not only through the Haight Ashbury crowd but all the way to Jack's platoon in Vietnam, where the LSD he had formulated and produced creating a new era of mind opening.

Nikki used the new guest's arrival to pull the three of them from the Vietnam debate that Jacks presence had generated. Nikki whispered in Jacks' ear, "I really want to introduce you to someone special." Nikki led the three of them into the back of the house.

Jack, I want you to meet Owsley "Bear" Stanley.

The three of them made small talk as Owsley handed Nikki a small Visine bottle.

"This is for you two," the guru of sound and psychedelia said. "Have fun."

Nikki held up the bottle. "LSD, Jack."

"Is that a dare?"

"Yes, it is, Jack."

He stuck out his tongue and Nikki administered each of them a generous drop.

She leaned in and whispered to Jack, "I want you in my bed."

The last girl he had made love to, he'd left dead on a floor in Vietnam.

CHAPTER TWENTY

Sherman hadn't heard from Bradley or Scott since they had left Ventura. His insecurities were starting to bleed into his daily existence. He had lost the bounce in his step. He had gotten severely dressed down by the chief and been told his efforts had been fruitless. In fact, since moving locations, the Question Marks had driven not only street criminals out of town but had eliminated several smaller bike clubs who were conducting themselves less than professionally. Some saw it as the Question Marks doing BET's job.

BET would remain intact, but they'd diversify. They would start investigating the growing drug problem plaguing the county. Oxnard was becoming a large heroin source, and something needed to be done. The chief told Sherman to get on it. Then, as he had done for years, he lifted Sherman back up.

"Get that started!" the chief told the sergeant. "And then pack a bag. You're meeting the feds in Cody, Wyoming."

Over the next week, Sherman briefed Cory while they worked on the local drug crackdown. They agreed they would start in Oxnard's La Colonia area. La Colonia was a tough neighborhood with a youth boxing club that had produced several world champions. But it also boasted Oxnard's oldest gang, East Side Colonia. They were a street faction that had ties to the Mexican Mafia, and they had to be taken seriously. This would be a covert operation. BET jackets would stay in the lockers at headquarters, but that didn't matter. Sherman had got his main target back in his sights, and the bounce back in his step.

Sherman received a message to call Ingram. Ingram told him to fly into Cody a day earlier than originally planned to be briefed by Bradley. The investigation, he was told, had taken on a life of its own. This meeting was on a need-to-know basis and very sensitive. Sherman understood.

The party had wound down, and the conversations had stopped hours ago, but Nikki and Jack continued on their journey, making their way to Nikki's house. They'd lost count of how many drops they each had taken long before they ventured out into the night. Time had escaped them, and they were now walking up a cobblestone walkway. They passed through a doorway, and a long narrow oriental rug welcomed them into this dark dimly lit hall. With each step, colorful sparks erupted off their shoes, helping to light their way. Jack had never been this high and asked Nikki if he was alright.

"Of course you are," she gently whispered to him. "We're together."

Nikki sat him down on a small bench at the end of the hall, helping him off with his boots and guiding him into the next room. His feet plunged deep into the carpet. His toes explored the surface. It was safe.

"Where are we?" he asked.

"At my house," she reminded him. "It's okay. Remember, you took a dare?"

All he could say was, "That's right."

And he was smiling.

Nikki put on one of the Bay Area underground radio shows. The tapestries and posters in her place came alive with lights and movement. Jack sat in silence and watched the show. Nikki appeared with tea and small slices of toast. Time was suspended. He started getting hot, and he kept taking off layers of his clothes. Nikki helped him and then helped herself.

On Jack's left chest was a tattoo: a view through the crosshairs of a sniper scope atop curved USMC block letters. Nikki looked at it intensely. Owsley's brew had a way of making everything more intense. Jack became uncomfortable with her stare and raised his forearm to cover his ink. But she pulled his arm away. "We have nothing to hide."

She removed her unbuttoned shirt and caressed her own perfect breasts.

"You see Jack. No secrets."

He tried to talk.

"No buts, Jack. That was then. This is now." She put her finger to his lips. "Shhh..."

Jack looked down between his legs. He was erect. He didn't even feel it. Nikki placed her left hand behind his neck and straddled him, lifting her body. With her other hand, she took two fingers and opened herself to him. She rode him gently until he came alive with passion. They didn't stop until the sun was high in the sky.

Sherman closed his eyes as the wheels of the plane folded up into the plane. He would be in Cody in a few hours. He contemplated if the investigation had truly taken on a life of its own, or if Bradley and Scott had given it one. Time to cover my own ass, he thought.

Bradley and Scott arrived mid-morning. Archie would travel by himself and arrive later. Scott was not excited about Sherman participating to this degree, but he had been overruled by the more experienced Ingram and Bradley.

Ingram and Bradley had decided that Archie would sit the first meeting out. It would take place at Cody police headquarters. If Keith was resistant, it would end there, and Archie would return home with as little exposure as possible.

Keith had been on several classified missions and would understand the responsibility that came along with this type of commitment, as a Marine and now as a cop. His obligation was to help. If he didn't, he wasn't doing his duty. And that's how they would sell this to him.

After introductions, Bradley did the talking. "Let me explain what brought us here. Do you recognize the location in these surveillance photos?"

One by one, Keith studied the photos.

"Ventura, California."

"Yes. You walked right into the middle of an investigation."

"It appears that way."

"What's your relationship with Jack Crest."

"Professional. We killed people."

That was enough for the meet and greet.

Bradley liked this guy. He set the next day's meeting for early morning. He wanted to get Archie out of town as quickly as possible.

The first thing Bradley noticed when they entered the meeting room for the second go-round was an addition: Keith's uncle was sitting at the table. Chief Parker nodded at Bradley but didn't acknowledge anyone else. Keith's father had gone MIA in Korea and Parker had become a surrogate dad to Keith. Parker was a good support to have—and an even greater reassurance for what Keith was doing.

Bradley got right to the point, with a question for Keith.

"Do you recognize this man?" he asked, pointing at Archie.

"No, I don't."

He did, but he chose a slight bit of evasion.

Bradley continued. "You were introduced to him as Archie, a Question Mark member. In fact, he is an ATF Agent who is deep undercover. We need to get Jack Crest off the street before he starts a street war that will be spread across the United States. What we want is for you to make several suppressed automatic weapons available to Mr. Crest. He's made several attempts to purchase weapons from Archie."

Keith interrupted. "It sounds like you don't need me as long as you've got him."

Keith looked at Archie.

"Yes, we do need you. Dealing with Archie alone would look as if we entrapped Crest. You're an independent."

Keith told them he wasn't comfortable with it.

"What team are you on?" interrupted Archie.

"I don't have to prove my loyalties."

"I think you do."

"Yeah? Well, fuck you!"

Bradley jumped in. "All we're asking is for you to reach out. Whether he bites or not, this will open many doors for you."

Keith looked at his uncle, who spoke deliberately. "It really comes down to what choice Crest makes. If he makes the wrong choice, he'll have to stand before the man. Crest knows that. He's a Marine. I say give it a one-time shot."

When Jack returned to the clubhouse from his "trip," Robert was waiting for him. Jack told him of his adventure and, like any good friend, Robert listened. But it was obvious, something was on his mind.

"What's bothering you?" Jack asked.

"That fucking Gypsy hung around all weekend."

"Doing what?"

"Packing anyone's nose who would listen to him."

"Yeah, he's in Archie's camp."

"He was more than in Archie's camp; he was recruiting his own army."

Jack and Robert decided they would say nothing but would keep an eye on Gypsy. Smokey and several Ventura members had listened, but that was the best Gypsy could do. Members weren't ready to get on a train that had no clear destination. Besides, no one was ready to test Jack. They had all heard the rumors.

Meanwhile, news about the attack on the clubhouse had circulated across the country. Not only with law enforcement but also in the outlaw bike world. The word in the East was that the Question Marks were thinking enough is enough. This is what caught Jimbo's and the other Orphans members' attention. And it hit the radar of one member in particular—Spike.

The Marks had Jack Crest; the Orphans had ex-Army Ranger Spike. Out of any conflict came men who killed to survive. They came home with a skill that others just didn't possess.

That gave them an edge. Spike was in his mid-twenties, average size and looks, but he was just plain too mean. He had burn marks and scars on his chest and back, but they weren't from the war. He had walked away from Vietnam without a scratch. His brands were something he had picked up from his long list of foster parents.

Spike didn't hide his anger well. When you opened the door to his home, his entrance was dedicated to his military service. It was a message of who this man was. In the center of the hallway was a large photo of him standing over a stack of VC heads in a perfect pyramid. In one hand he held a large knife, in the other, a pistol. And there was a smile on his face.

Jimbo okayed the trip to Ventura, but it was really Spike's show. This trip would be just reconnaissance. When the war kicked off, it would not be just in the East. Spike would take it to the West Coast, and to Jack Crest.

Jack answered his phone and was caught off guard.

"Do you recognize my voice?"

"Yes."

Jack was smart enough to know Keith didn't want his name put out over the phone. He just wasn't sure why.

"I'm in town. Can I see you?"

"Yes. Where?"

"Chrystal Lodge."

"Give me ten minutes."

Jack hung up the phone, and that now-too-familiar feeling hit him. He started to sweat and had to fight to hold down what was in his stomach. The upper part of his legs became heavy and pushed on his knees, making them weak. He gathered himself and went to the sink in the kitchen and threw cold water on his face.

Don't go, he told himself. But he laughed that off, knowing it wasn't even an option.

Robert had never seen Jack anything but composed. But now he looked wet and pasty white.

"Damn! You okay?"

"Yeah. Must be something I ate."

Robert didn't believe him. His first thought was that goddamn reporter, Nikki. She was starting to take up all of Jack's time. Maybe even getting in his head, and Robert wasn't the only one who didn't like her taking up Jack's attention.

Jack told Robert he'd be right back and abruptly made his exit. Robert watched as he drove off in his truck.

Jack pulled into the Chrystal Lodge's lot and saw Keith standing in front of a room, smoking. Keith only smoked when he was nervous. That stood out as Jack assessed the scene.

"What the hell is going on Keith?"

"Let's go inside."

Jack watched as Keith field-stripped his cigarette, and then led the way into his room.

"What's the big mystery?"

"I have a business proposition for you."

"What would that be?"

"I have a dozen Ruger Mini-14s with selective fire."

"What would I do with them?"

"That's your business, Jack."

"Jesus Christ. What are you doing, Keith? You're a cop!"

"They fell into my hands, so to speak. It's a one-time deal for me."

"I'm not going to take you down that road. Find someone else. Better yet, forget it!"

Jack was tempted, sure. But it just didn't feel right.

Keith had never been the nervous type like he seemed here and now. Something just didn't fit.

"I'm going to pass on this."

"So, that's it—no interest?"

"No. In fact, I'm going to leave, and the next time we see each other, this never happened. See you down the road, Keith."

With that, Jack walked out and didn't look back.

Keith made no attempt to stop Jack as relief ran through his body. He had been pressured into this, but that didn't make it right. And he knew it. It was something he was going to have to come to terms with along with all the other baggage from his past.

There was a loud banging on the door that connected to the adjoining room. In the next room, Bradley, Scott, and Sherman had heard every word. They had struck out again.

"That was a goddamn piss poor performance," barked Scott.

"Fuck you. I did what you asked, and he didn't bite."

"Next time you—"

"There is no next time," interrupted Keith. "I took my shot."

"Yeah, maybe. But it was a fucking misfire."

The exchange went on for several minutes. Allegations and accusations back and forth. On a table in the adjoining room, the reel to reel continued to record the exchange.

Bradley offered Keith another one of his Turkish cigarettes. He extended him a light and then walked over to the table and turned off the recorder. Bradley had hoped things would go better but was satisfied that Keith had even participated. He now felt he had his hooks in him for future operations. But he chose not to share this with anyone in the room.

What had just happened?

Jack felt like the walls were closing in on him in the cab of the pickup. The thought of going back to his room at the clubhouse was claustrophobic. He gravitated to Nikki's place in the foothills of Ventura, the only solace he had found as of late.

When Jack abruptly woke out of a deep sleep, he and the sheets were soaked from his night sweats, the first in months. And he had called out in his sleep and woken Nikki.

She tried to comfort him. "You called for Keith."

"I did?"

"Who is Keith?"

"I'm not really sure."

And he really wasn't anymore. He told Nikki to get on top of the covers. The bed was wet. He covered her with a blanket and told her to sleep.

Jack didn't know if it was a dream or vision, but he had seen Keith field-stripping one of Bradley's Turkish cigarettes. All he knew was that he had seen Keith do it a few hours earlier. It made sense.

Of course, Bradley had gotten to Keith.

Jack took a towel from the bathroom and dried off before getting dressed.

He made his way back to the Chrystal Lodge. He parked on the side street. He moved through the early morning darkness to Keith's room. There were no cars out front. He stood at the door to the room listening. No sounds. He tried to insert his knife between the door and the jam just above the doorknob.

Too wide. He pulled out his smaller penknife. The thin blade caught the plunger. He pushed it in and opened the door slowly. No door chain. Jack now had his fixed blade knife at the ready. He held it in what some knife fighters call an ice-pick position, blade facing out. He could slash or insert depending on body position.

Jack was relieved that the room was empty, but the door that separated the room from the one next door was ajar. Light from the adjoining room was bleeding into Keith's room. Jack stopped, listened, then looked.

Empty.

In the middle of the room was a coffee table. The ashtray was full of cigarettes, some Turkish. The same cigarettes Keith had been smoking several hours earlier. The beds in both rooms had not been slept in. By the drinking glasses and the trash, it appeared there had been three to four people in the rooms.

Jack sat on the end of the bed, lost in thought. He put his knife back in its sheath. The sun would be up soon. He slipped back into the darkness.

At the clubhouse, Robert was sitting at the bar. They nodded at each other.

"What you doing up?" Jack asked.

"I didn't want to miss you. Your lawyer's secretary called. You have a four o'clock appointment tomorrow."

"You mean today."

"You know what the fuck I mean."

They both laughed as Robert poured two shots of tequila.

Jack toasted Robert. "To friendship."

Bradley and Scott said their goodbyes to Sherman and told him they would be in touch. They made what was becoming an all-too-familiar trip back to the airport.

Bradley looked over at Scott. "That Crest is a slippery fuck."

Scott thought for a moment. "Let's send Archie back out here."

"Not yet," Bradley told him. "Let's hold off. The pressure is going to build for Crest to do something. He wanted those rifles. I heard it in his voice. Let Archie keep working."

Archie had built several cases in the East. He was selling, buying, and trading guns with several Question Marks, as well as prospects. They were all preparing for the war that was sure to come. He made no attempt at narcotics purchases. That would be on his agenda during his next trip west. Gypsy would be the source and the root for a national drug conspiracy to fund a war.

Archie had developed a close relationship with Gypsy. He had gotten high with him. He hadn't planned on using, but it just happened. He even wrote up a report explaining the circumstances. When it crossed Bradley's desk, he made sure all the copies were destroyed. Then he got Archie's head right.

That little party never happened.

Jack made the appointment on time. He knew Glen wasn't the type of man you kept waiting. Glen often had written reports for Jack, but not this time. Glen greeted him and got right to the point.

"You may have a problem." He looked Jack in the eyes. Jack chose not to interrupt. "Does the name Jimmy 'Spike' Smith mean anything to you?"

Jack shook his head no.

Glen continued, "I have several addresses, none of which I believe he actually resides in. All are back east. Ex-Army Ranger. What will interest you is that he was stopped here in Ventura and given a ticket a few weeks back. He had an Orphan tattoo on his right inside forearm. I didn't want to take this any further until we talked. What do you want me to do?"

"I'll take it from here."

Glen said he understood. He also indicated a folder on the desk. He suggested Jack take a look at it before he left. Glen did not return to the office until Jack was gone.

Back at the clubhouse, Jack put in a call to Silent Bob to confirm who Spike was. Jack chose not to let Bob know too much. He just wanted confirmation that Spike was indeed an Orphan.

CHAPTER TWENTY-ONE

0600.

Spike, the attack on the clubhouse, Glen's file, and most of all Jack's haunting past, had brought him to this perch in the desert.

Jack was now waiting for Jimbo to enter the sights of his scope. Robert watched through a pair of field glasses. Jack noticed that Robert was breathing a little heavy and hoped he had not made a mistake in bringing him. The first kill is always the hardest, he thought.

If Jack could have been inside the house he was watching, he would have seen not much difference between the Orphans and the Question Marks.

The members.

The girls.

The conversations.

Jimbo sat in a chair at the kitchen table eating his breakfast. He made the trip out to the Walker Ranch almost every harvest. The vehicle with the weed had left hours ago. Jimbo would be leaving soon.

Jack's mind began to wander again. How the fuck does Glen find out these things? He wondered. Goddamn, he realized, I wonder who's watching me?

He cleared his head and went back to waiting.

Jack and Robert had made just one stop on their way to this corner of the California desert: Old Man John's warehouse in Santa Paula. John provided a car, three full five-gallon gas cans, two dress suits, and several wigs to choose from. The weapons were hidden in a false floor under the rear seat. They hung the two suit jackets on the back seat garment hooks. They each had on a white shirt and black tie. Just a couple of salesmen on the road. John never asked where they were going or said goodbye.

Based on Glen's intel, Jack had taken a trip out here a week earlier on a rice rocket, wearing a blue leather riding suit and a matching full-face helmet. No one took a second look at him. Just an innocent sport-bike jockey out for some high- speed fun on an empty highway. That's what those guys had always done.

Jack had found a long surface road that cut down their five-mile hike by half. Less than a mile before the turn-off, he spray-painted a large black X in the opposite road lane. It was necessary—all these surface roads looked exactly the same.

Jack and Robert had found the X and turned onto the surface road, driving right to the spot Jack had scouted a week earlier.

They'd ditched the wigs and the suits for the more field-type dress. They disconnected the ground wire from the battery and emptied the gas cans into the tank. Jack wanted that car right there and ready when they returned. And they would not stop until they were well out of the area.

Then they started their hump to the Walker Ranch. About a half-mile in, they stopped. Jack took the E-Tool he had been carrying, opened it up, and dug a nice-sized hole in the sandy desert surface. Then he unzipped the large canvas bag he was carrying and removed the items. Robert took the suppressed MAC-10, several magazines, field glasses, and a canteen. Jack took the rifle, a handgun, several clips, a compass, and an additional canteen. They each had a small soft backpack with a long underwear top, light jacket, some rations, and snakebite kit.

They got to the spot right after dark.

A ladder was still lying on the ground near the barn. It looked like the roof repairs hadn't been finished. Tough break for Jimbo, Jack thought. It made getting up on that roof way too easy.

The moon and stars lit up the night sky. Once their eyes adjusted, his and Robert's night vision was good. Jack felt excellent. He was at home again.

The peak of the roof where he positioned himself was about three hundred yards from the target. He had fired the rifle several times up in Rose Valley, above Ojai. He was confident he would hit his mark. It wouldn't be much longer. The sun was on the rise.

In the house, Jimbo finished breakfast. He was on his second cup of coffee when he told a prospect to take the bags to the car. It was an older black Lincoln, parked at an odd angle about fifty feet from the front door. Not so much a limo, the car was more the type used at funeral homes to transport family members to and from cemeteries.

The prospect exited the front door of the house with a bag in each hand. He made his way to the big car and opened the trunk. He put in each bag and then climbed behind the wheel and cranked the ignition. It rumbled to life, the twin glass packs just a little bit loud.

Jack saw this as ironic; the funeral transport car would be a fitting end for Jimbo.

He spoke out loud, as much to himself as to Robert, "We're on."

Jack started controlling his breath as he waited. He was impressed with Robert. They had a pre-determined plan of operation, and Robert followed it to the letter. He moved to the eave and made his way down the ladder. He would provide cover fire if needed. Robert made his way to the corner of the barn and took his position. But Jack was sure it would be chaos, then panic, and then a quick exit. They would be long gone after the shot, back into the desert and safety.

Jimbo rose from the table.

As always, he had the last word. "Let's roll."

Everyone snapped to attention and focused on their leader. Jimbo was respected, but more than that he was feared. Over the years, more than one Orphan who became an obstacle had suddenly disappeared. It was rumored Jimbo had originally taken over the club at gunpoint. He had gone around the room, from member to member, extricating those who didn't make the cut.

"You're okay … you leave it on the table … you stay, you beat it..."

And so the story went.

The prospect opened the door and then stepped aside. With his entourage in tow, Jimbo's massive frame filled the space that only moments ago was a full-sized doorway.

Jack sighted him in.

Jimbo walked out into the morning sun. Jack adjusted and said a personal touching goodbye to Jimbo: "Sorry about that." His favorite Marine Corps saying that had become his assassination mantra before each shot.

But Jack captured the second figure over Jimbo's left shoulder.

Panic filled his thoughts. Jack raised the scope up, and at about forty-five degrees, he saw a woman who could have passed for the last person he shot and killed in Vietnam.

Jack's superstition overtook his thoughts. This was a sign.

What he was doing was a mistake. He didn't take the shot. He watched Jimbo, and the woman, whose name he would learn later was "China Lady," drive off in the Lincoln. It rocked as it moved forward and out of Jack's view.

Robert was in a panic and had come very close to charging the car and spraying it with his weapon.

Too late.

He stayed in his cover position as he watched Jack descend the ladder.

"Let's go!" Jack told him.

"What happened?"

"It wasn't right, and that's all I want to say."

They made their way back through the desert. When they got to the hole they had dug on their way out, Jack told Robert to make a nondescript marker to locate the spot. Jack field stripped the weapons, wiped them down with oil and rolled them in plastic. He put them in the zipper bag and placed them in the hole. Jack took the folding shovel and covered the bag and its contents with the desert. Robert hooked the battery cable back up and got behind the wheel.

There was very little in the way of conversation on the way home.

CHAPTER TWENTY-TWO

Bill Bradley sat in his office smoking. Not many people got close to Bradley. If they had, they would have recognized he was displaying his pose of deep contemplation; holding his cigarette in an odd way, between his thumb and index fingers stained yellow from years of smoking unfiltered cigarettes, palm inward and up toward his face.

To dispose of the ash, he would extend his forearm, turn his palm downward, and twist counter-clockwise. One snapping twisting motion down, then back up for the next draw on his exotic blend of tobacco.

Fourteen months had passed since Bradley's first conversation with Jack. He thought how foolish Crest had been to reject the government's overture. Bradley had helped facilitate the demise of better men than him, others who had chosen to go down that road of non-compliance.

Jack Crest was nothing compared to those men. So why, Bradley asked himself, has this vagrant on a motorcycle got so into my head? Everyone makes a mistake sooner or later. Was this his own?

He quickly moved on from that thought. Bradley went back

to his blackboard of photos, maps, and dates tying the operation together. They had reached the last chapter of this operation.

Archie's undercover work would soon pay dividends. Dozens of indictments would be handed down by a federal grand jury. They would try their hardest in these next few weeks to make sure that one had Jack Crest's name on it. At the very least, they would paint him to the federal grand jury with the same brush as his associates. And hope for a true bill vote against him.

For Bob Ingram, this was just another assignment. Spending as little time in the field as possible served a dual purpose. It limited his exposure, as well as ensuring that he had little or no emotional connection to the events that transpired.

Ingram was an analyst; the individual who had shifted through the stacks of reports. After sterilizing them, he returned them to the agents through Bradley. Ingram fixed any and all of Archie's actions that were borderline questionable or outright misconduct. Ingram was the one who decided which taped conversations would be destroyed and which would be submitted.

He organized all the evidence into a chronological order of criminal behavior. When he was satisfied with the story it told, it was he and he alone who made the decision: It was time to move toward the indictments.

Ingram was the referee calling the fight.

More than one of the personnel involved in this investigation suspected that Bradley threw the grenade into the Ventura Question Marks clubhouse.

Ingram knew it.

He'd followed the serial numbers on the spoon from the police reports out of Ventura. Turns out, Bradley had been given a case of grenades from that very lot number to infiltrate the radical-left organization, the Weathermen. Bradley had gone from college campus to college campus making contacts with as many militant organizations as possible.

Ingram chuckled aloud in his office at the thought of how many of those grenades Bradley still possessed. Ingram thought it best to keep Bill Bradley a friend.

ATF Agent Scott was ready to put all this behind him. It wasn't so much the sticky morality of the investigation, but the tedious preparation for the trial that would follow. A long and brutal court battle would surely be fought. He wondered how many defendants and how many U.S. Attorneys would fill the courtroom. He had managed to stay in the shadows up to this point, but this investigation and subsequent trial would take all that away.

He imagined how he would address all the questions at the press conferences that would take place. He even practiced aloud, his image reflected back at him from the mirror, answering with rapid-fire statements of fact. He would surely have a daily place at the U.S. prosecutor's table. He had been told that this was the type of case that made careers.

Indeed it was.

Scott would be able to write his own ticket. Everyone, in this case, knew that this was a team effort. But in the end, there was really only one star. Scott had done a good job hiding his envy toward Archie.

Archie lay in his bed staring at the ceiling. He was sleeping less and less each night. He wanted to blame it on the case, but deep down he knew it was his continued drug use that was the issue.

But that subject was taboo, with everyone ignoring what was happening in front of them. Everyone had come too far to let a small misstep like drug use interfere with this major operation.

Ingram and Bradley had discussed the problem and knew they were running out of time. They knew Archie was tampering with meth, a powerful drug with emotional highs and lows, and it was starting to affect his actions. So they decided that Archie would return to Ventura one last time. Take one more shot at Jack Crest and then ride his bike home.

Archie had talked Gypsy into riding back east with him, but not as a riding partner; even though that was the cover story.

Gypsy would venture east to teach Archie the art of cooking drugs. Gypsy had obtained most of what was needed. It had all been shipped and was awaiting his arrival on the East Coast.

Archie would supply the hard-to-locate P2P—pheny1-2-propanone— thanks to Bradley. Gypsy would cook the drugs and then help distribute them through Archie.

These acts would give the feds their national conspiracy; not with the acts of violence they had initially sought, but with narcotics manufacturing and sales. It was their second choice but just as good. And maybe even a better story for the media.

This would end the fieldwork of the investigation. Archie knew this would also be the end of his street career.

The payoff, however, would be well worth it.

He imagined himself as the premier undercover agent, lecturing recruits as well as agents who were getting ready to take on the most dangerous job in law enforcement. He would travel the country as a consultant. He had been keeping a secret log that would be the outline for the author who would ghost write his story. The possibilities were endless.

Sherman received what amounted to a simple courtesy call from Scott. He was informed that the feds would be in the area, in all likelihood for the final time—for this particular investigation, anyway.

Scott would advise him of the time frame once it was locked in. He made no mention of coordinating or meeting with the BET.

Well, big deal, Sherman thought. These are the best the feds have got? Not impressed. They should have gone after these thugs state by state and county by county. If they had left it to the locals, that fucking Jack Crest would be off the streets right now and the Question Marks on the run. All this worthless running around from state to state. The strategy meetings that netted nothing. If it weren't for their ability to write that big check, he would have kicked their federal asses out of town months ago, Chief or no Chief. Fuck 'em!

Jack got behind the wheel after he and Robert burned through the first tank of gas. When they hit Ventura, Jack drove past the 126 exit that would have taken them back to Santa Paula.

Robert looked over at Jack. Was there a change of plans?

"I want to show you something," Jack told him.

Jack pulled into his fishing spot just as the sun was getting ready to set. It was big and red-orange. The water was like glass, and as the sun plunged into the ocean, it looked like steam was rising off the water, extinguishing the big ball of fire.

"Have you ever killed anyone?" Jack gazed over the water as he asked it.

The question caught Robert off guard. "No, I haven't."

"I hope you never have to."

There was an uncomfortable pause. Then Jack spoke again.

"When you kill the body, the souls don't know where to go. So they just follow you around. They think you can help them. But you can't."

"Jesus Christ Jack. Is that what happened in the desert?"

"I don't really know. Maybe. It just wasn't right."

"It was your call, Jack. I'm not judging."

"I'm not thinking about that. I think that the Orphans had nothing to do with the attack. I think we can talk things out."

"You don't think it's too late?"

"If it is, we can always go back out to that ranch. I want to at least try. Our problem is with law enforcement, not bike people. My thinking is one country, one club."

"Come on Jack. That ain't gonna happen."

"I'm willing to try."

The pair sat on the rocks as the red sky dimmed.

They watched the sun set. The same sun they'd watched rise that morning many miles away.

The drive to Santa Paula took about thirty minutes. In silence, it felt twice that long.

John was happy the car was back in one piece; it was one of the few late-model cars the company owned. It would have been hard to explain to Mr. Hayward.

The old man didn't say anything—or ask—but he walked around the car looking for damage. More specifically, bullet holes.

Jack laughed. "Did it pass inspection?"

"It's my ass on the line, Jack!"

"Yes, and we took good care of it."

Jack asked if the old man had a couple minutes to talk. Robert wandered into the warehouse to find Dick Woods.

"I want to have a sit-down with Jimbo and the Orphans."

"Are you asking me or telling me? Because you're a leader now. You should be telling me."

"I've already made up my mind."

"Okay. What do you think you can accomplish?"

"Stop us from destroying each other and leaving the winner for the cops to dismantle." Jack was silent a moment and then stated the obvious. "It's not going to be popular."

"A good leader doesn't choose what's popular. He does what's best for everyone concerned. Are you that leader?"

"I think I am."

"You better be sure, Jack. You're going to get challenged every step of the way."

"I'm just going to set it up and deal with the fallout later."

"That's smart. If you don't, Archie will make sure that meeting never happens."

"I hate that motherfucker."

"You've made that more than clear—to everyone."

"I need you to do something for me, John."

"What would that be?"

"After I meet with Jimbo, I'll call you. I want you to call Silent Bob and ask him to tell the East Coast that I met with Jimbo. Ask Bob to stand down and then set up a tentative meeting at our clubhouse."

"I can do that," the old man told Jack. "But it'll be his choice what he does."

"I know," said Jack. "But at least he'll listen to you."

CHAPTER TWENTY-THREE

Nikki pulled into the small parking lot of a rundown restaurant. It didn't surprise her. It was either one or the other with Jack: top of the line or bottom of the barrel.

The Japanese restaurant sign was faded, like the paint on the rest of the building. By the layout, it had likely been a drive-in burger place sometime back in the fifties.

Jack was standing by his bike, and the large Question Mark emblem on his vest jumped out at her, defying everything that society had based its universal order around. Even Nikki had begun to question whether they were just displaced outcasts from society, or if they were transitioning into a well-oiled crime syndicate.

Several days earlier, Nikki had been called into her editor's office. A man in a wrinkled suit sat in the chair across from her boss. He was a small man, and his eyes blinked continually as they jumped around the room. His small hand displayed a class ring. It took Nikki a bit to make out the letters that spelled "Annapolis."

The man introduced himself as Robert Maxwell—one of Bob Ingram's many aliases. He pivoted on his cover story after noticing

Nikki's interest in his ring. He said he was a retired military analyst who was now an independent criminal consultant and analyst for law enforcement. Nikki took the chair next to him, turned it forty-five degrees to him, and sat.

"So basically, you're a hired gun?"

"Well, I've been called worse."

His dry humor had never gotten him far with women. Neither had his looks.

"What can I do for you?"

"It's what I can do for you."

"And what would that be, Mr. Maxwell?"

"An exclusive inside story—with a condition, of course."

"That's always the problem with you law enforcement types. You're the ones who want to be in control. My loyalties are to the public, not law enforcement."

"Hear him out, Nikki," said the editor. "This could be big. I expect it to get picked up over the wire."

"We anticipate arrests across the country," Ingram told her. "This will go national, and you'll break this story. We know from your past pieces that you're familiar with the Question Marks. It was good journalism but slanted to the wrong team. Once you know the truth, you'll do the right thing."

For the next couple of hours, Ingram wove a story of murder, mayhem, and a national drug conspiracy. It was the story of an emerging criminal empire with Jack Crest—the man she was in love with—at the helm.

Nikki tried to maintain her composure, but she became flushed. Her first thought was that they were toying with her.

But as the story continued, she realized they were not; and somehow her relationship with Jack had gone completely undetected by law enforcement.

Jack was happy to see Nikki. She called him immediately after her discussion with "Maxwell." She really needed to talk—face-to-face.

Still smiling, Jack said, "You said we needed to find an 'out of the way' place."

"Well, yes,_but is it safe to eat here?"

"You bet! Try the dog; it's great!"

They entered the restaurant, and Mama-san greeted them. "You sit here, Jack. Oh, new lady friend! Very nice!"

"What ya got tonight, San-san?"

"You have two teriyaki chicken."

"Let's see the menu tonight."

"No. No menu. You eat chicken."

"And a bowl of noodle soup."

"No soup; just chicken!"

At the table next to them, a woman tried to get an additional order to go as she was finishing her meal. San-san informed her in broken English that she'd waited too long to order and to try again next time. A young man at the counter ordered a large to-go order and was bluntly told to go wait outside; that she didn't like his attitude. Then she added, "Next time have someone else come to order!"

The food was that good, and this was just the show that went on every night they were open.

"Is this for real?"

"As real as they come."

"And how about you, Jack Crest?"

Jack looked into Nikki's face when he heard the question. He noticed that her voice was different; it was an actual question.

"What the hell does that mean?"

"It was a simple question. Ever kill anyone?"

"Have you?"

"With kindness, maybe," she replied.

"What kind of thing is that to ask someone?"

"You made it seem like it was a topic open for discussion in Berkeley."

"But this isn't Berkeley, is it?"

"You know, you're right. Let's start over. Why would so many people say so many bad things about you?"

"I think you ought to be asking them."

"Oh, believe me—I don't have to ask. They're more than happy to tell me all about you."

"So, then, you don't want to see me anymore."

"I didn't say that."

"What the hell are you saying?"

"Convince me you're not a bad guy," she pleaded, wanting all those things swimming around in her head to be wrong.

"Am I on trial?"

"You know what, you're right. That's out of line."

"I thought you knew me, or at least had an idea who I am." Jack couldn't understand what had gone wrong.

Before anything else could be said, San-san brought their dinners. She obviously felt the vibe at the table. She made a sour face at them and said, "You eat, you feel better."

Nikki stared at Jack. "If you are doing something wrong— let's say something illegal—I would stop."

Jack stared right back. "Is that a dare?"

Nikki whispered, "Yes, it is."

Bob Ingram had slipped in and out of Ventura so quickly no one was the wiser. After all, it wasn't really Ingram who had made the trip; it was Robert Maxwell.

Sherman was never contacted. Ingram didn't realize that his failure to include Sherman was a mistake. If Sherman had been included, a different reporter and newspaper would have been chosen to break the story. Sherman had witnessed Jack and Nikki walking together on the streets of downtown Ventura.

The suspicion the agencies harbored for each other had benefited the target of the investigation. Far worse than inter-agency suspicions are the personalities involved who are looking for their own glory.

Jack stood by a pay phone feeding quarters into the machine for long-distance charges. He was working off a list Glen had put together for him and was on his third call. Call number one had gotten him a "Fuck you," and the second one, a "Call later, motherfucker." Jack paused, thinking how to improvise. He needed something more.

He soon came up with a game plan.

He knew about an Orphans patch that the old man had been holding onto for years. That would open the conversation. Jack watched the dial spin back to its starting point after he chose each number. He waited. The deep voice on the other end answered with a single greeting.

"Clubhouse."

"I'm trying to get a message to Jimbo."

"What would that be?"

"I have some Orphan property I want to return to him."

"Who is this?" the voice asked suspiciously.

Time to take the gamble: "Jack Crest, Ventu—"

"I know who you are," the voice on the other end interrupted him.

Jack wasn't sure if that was a good thing or not. He hoped he had made the right decision.

"Give me fifteen minutes. What's your callback number?"

Jack read out the numbers one by one. The voice on the other end read them back slow and deliberately. Jack told the person he would wait for the fifteen.

Jack looked at his watch then at Robert.

Then Jack asked, "Who am I talking to?"

"You're talking to Spike."

"Okay—Spike."

They both hung up.

The next fifteen minutes felt like fifteen hours. Jack let the phone ring three times before he lifted the receiver.

"Yeah."

"Jack Crest?"

"Yes."

"So, I hear you have something that belongs to me."

"I do if you're Jimbo."

"I'm listening."

"I have an Orphans patch."

You could feel the surprise over the line. "How did you come across one of our cuts?"

"A girl traveling through Ventura; she was out of Chicago."

"How can I get it?"

"I'll bring it to you."

"Why would you do that?"

"Because I think we need to talk."

Keith had been moody and sullen since his conversation with Jack in the cheap Ventura motel room. He had always held camaraderie in the highest regard. But now, not only had he betrayed his friend but even worse than that, he had betrayed his own beliefs and himself.

He'd started drinking on the plane ride back to Cody and hadn't really stopped. Sure, he would slow down enough to function at work and when he was in the reserve unit. But every night would end in an alcoholic blackout. Every morning, or sometimes the afternoon, he would methodically try to piece back together the events that had disappeared into the mystery of the previous night.

His uncle had seen enough. Chief Parker waited for Keith as he pulled into the police station parking lot. He stepped into the path of the unit and stopped it. He climbed into the passenger seat and told his nephew to drive.

"Where to?"

Barely holding in anger, he told Keith, "Just drive."

After a few moments of awkward silence, he launched into Keith. "What the hell is going on with you? You have been FUBAR since you got back from California. You need to square your ass away and put that trip behind you. If that fucking Crest has gone sideways, that's his problem, not yours. You said he didn't bite, so what's the fucking problem? Has life hit you between your running lights?" Keith hadn't had a good military ass chewing since boot camp and knew his uncle, boss, and the military commander had had enough. It was time to get right.

"It was wrong."

"No, it was a fucking mission. You took it, and now it's over. That Crest is no dummy. I'm sure he knows he's a target. You need to get your ass out from behind that eight ball. Do we understand each other?"

"Aye aye, sir!"

Jack and Robert arrived in Chicago forty-eight hours before the scheduled meeting with Jimbo. They grabbed a shuttle and got a motel room near the airport. Then they took a taxi to a used car lot to purchase an unassuming sedan. This would give them control over their movements and a way out if things went south. Jack was also planning a couple of stops on the trip home. Jack told Robert it would allow them to kill two birds with one stone. They both laughed. They picked up a local map and familiarized themselves with city streets and exit paths. Not only to the west but to the east as well.

The meeting was on Orphan turf, but Jack would choose the location. He considered the airport, beyond the security gates. This would ensure that no one was armed. But he decided against it. There were too many cameras and too many cops in that small secure area.

Jack noticed a large conference room at the Airport Holiday Inn. He slipped the desk clerk fifty bucks to use it. He inspected the room and studied the hotel map layout.

It was perfect.

Jack called Jimbo and gave him the location and time where they would meet. Jack had made it clear to Jimbo that he and Robert had flown in from LAX and just the two of them would be at the meeting. Jimbo informed Jack that it didn't matter to him how many Question Marks came. He would have a total of six Orphans in two cars. Four in one vehicle and two who would stay in a backup vehicle in the parking lot. They agreed there would be no patches at the meeting except the Orphan patch that would be returned to Jimbo.

There was no mention, however, of weapons.

Agent Scott didn't have much interest in the phone ringing until he picked it up and recognized his former partner's voice. They'd kept in touch, and each had a basic knowledge of what type of cases the other was currently involved in. His old partner was now working organized crime in Chicago.

After a brief catch-up conversation, Scott asked the point of the call. He was told that the Orphans had been performing collections for a large bookie operation, and a confidential informant had passed on information that there was going to be a sit-down in Chicago between two bike clubs: the Question Marks and the Orphans.

Scott's old comrade said that was all the information he had for now, but if he received any more intel, he would pass it on. Scott thanked him, adding that he was very interested in any more details that might turn up.

Scott had to weigh out the situation carefully. His first concern was for Archie's safety. Archie had checked in less than two hours ago but had made no mention of any meeting between the Question Marks and Orphans. Scott couldn't help but wonder if Archie had been left out of the loop because he had been compromised. Or was this possibly some sort of timeline glitch?

What Scott needed was time to think.

Jack and Robert stood in front of the hotel entrance and waited. A pickup truck pulled into the lot, the bed covered with a dirty canvas tarp. It backed into a parking space, and Jack could see that it held two men. They didn't get out but settled into their seats. Jack could feel that behind their dark sunglasses, their eyes were trained on him and Robert.

Waiting to turn into the lot was the same black Lincoln they had seen in the desert.

Jack smiled at Robert. "I wonder who that is."

They both chuckled softly, but Jack had the fleeting thought, What the hell am I laughing at? I fucking choked, and he told himself that there was nothing to laugh at. Jack gathered himself and walked to the center of the lot to greet the envoy car that carried the Orphan leader.

Jimbo's massive body caused the limo to rock from side to side as he exited the car. Standing next to him, Jack thought first how much smaller he had looked through the scope. But now, Jack liked what he saw—and more so—what he felt from this man he had come very close to killing. You could tell Jimbo was impressed as well. And not just with Jack. Robert stood to the right of his leader's shoulder and back a half a step. The Orphans could see there was no fear in these two men from California.

Jack spoke first and handed Jimbo the folded Orphans patch with his left hand as he extended his right hand. "I'm Jack Crest. This is Robert."

Jimbo accepted the folded Orphans property without inspecting it as he extended his hand and introduced the man next to him as Spike. Jack wasn't sure how he felt about this ex-Army Ranger. Jack noticed that they both had on bulletproof vests.

After the introductions, the four men walked into the lobby of the Holiday Inn. Two of the four Orphans in the Lincoln stayed back with the car; more backup added to the two in the pickup.

Jimbo, Spike, Robert, and Jack proceeded into the conference room. Near the center of the room stood a table with four chairs. An additional table off to the side held coffee, pastries, and a pitcher of water with cups and glasses.

The four men started to take their seats, but when Jimbo leaned into the chair, a black semi-auto pistol fell out of his coat onto the floor. All four men tensed.

Jack broke the silence. "I didn't know we were bringing guns?"

Jimbo looked into Jack's eyes and replied, "That's not for you."

"Then why don't you put it away?" Jack calmly asked.

Everyone at the table smiled at Jack's suggestion. Jimbo carefully picked up the weapon in a non-threatening manner and placed it back in his jacket.

Jack then began to speak. “I think the main thing that separates our two clubs is geography.”

Jimbo thought for a moment. “So you don’t think you’re better than us?”

“No, not at all,” Jack responded. “But I’m happy with where I’m at. I will tell you this, though. I bet if I lived in Chicago I would be an Orphan and there is no doubt in my mind that if you lived in California, you’d be a Question Mark.”

“That so?” said Jimbo.

Jack nodded. “We have a common enemy,” he continued.

“Who would that be?”

“Law enforcement. You must realize that if we don’t find a way to co-exist, they’re going to pick apart, piece by piece, whoever is left standing.”

The room fell silent for several seconds.

“I’m open to change,” Jimbo admitted, “but this is a lot.”

“We have to start small,” said Jack. “This is a beginning.”

Jimbo looked from Jack to Robert, and then at Spike. “Well, I have to tell you, I have some unhappy members right now.”

“Well, so do I,” replied Jack. “But do they really know what they’re unhappy about?”

“Maybe that’s not important anymore.”

“I think it is,” argued Jack. “And I’m not saying this can end overnight.”

"That's good because it can't," Jimbo smirked.

Jack took a deep breath and went on, "I know that. We need to start with an open line of communication. Stop all the rumors floating around. And that's why I have to ask you this question: Do the Orphans know anything about the grenade that was thrown into our clubhouse?"

"If I said no, would you believe me?"

"I would give you the benefit of the doubt."

Jimbo looked each man in the eyes. "Let's just say there are several Question Marks' targets much closer to us than Ventura."

Nodding his understanding, Jack replied, "Okay then, let's move on from that."

The conversation went back and forth for another hour.

Several logistical issues were discussed, and both factions agreed to at least a temporary stand-down order.

As the meeting broke up and they all shook hands, Jack couldn't resist letting Spike know that his recent movements had not gone unnoticed. "Hey, the next time you're in Ventura, we should have dinner. I know all the good spots."

Spike replied with no hesitation. "Only if you're buying."

The four of them exchanged direct numbers and then said their goodbyes. As soon as the Lincoln left, Jack went to the lobby desk and settled the bill. Robert made his way back to the meeting room and retrieved the two pistols taped to the underside of the meeting table. He pulled out his shirt from his waistband

and placed one in the small of his back. He stuffed the other in his front waist. He pulled his shirt over them and went to the car and waited.

Jack made the call to Old Man John and told him he felt good about the meeting and to go ahead and get in touch with Silent Bob. He let John know they would be driving back and to give them a couple of days.

To Robert's surprise, Jack didn't head west, but south to Indianapolis. Within the hour, Jack was counting on all the Question Mark charters to have heard about the meeting. He was betting that Archie would head to Silent Bob's in Omaha and then to California for the proposed meeting.

Agent Scott picked up the phone on the first ring. The voice on the other end said, "It's me."

"Goddamn, I was getting worried."

"That fucking Crest just met with Jimbo from the Orphans."

"I know. Why were you left out of the loop?"

"He left the whole goddamn club out of the loop. He thinks it's his club. I'm on my way to Omaha and then to Ventura."

"So you're safe."

"Yes."

"You're positive?"

"I'll be riding back with Gypsy, as planned."

"I'll call Bradley; stay in touch."

Jack's calculation was correct. When he and Robert drove by Archie's house, it was dark. There were no lights on, just a dim porch light. Jack had Robert stop around the corner. All Robert asked was if Jack was sure this is what he wanted to do. Jack said he wasn't, but he was going to do it anyway. He took one of the guns and a small flashlight and went in through the back door.

Jack immediately felt that the whole house had a staleness to it. It was empty of anything that might have made it comfortable, and it didn't feel or smell like it was lived in. Jack thought about his own personal space and realized his room could be described in the same terms.

He didn't find much in the refrigerator or the cupboards. A stack of mail sat on the table. Jack pulled out one of the chairs and took a seat and thumbed through the pile, but he found nothing of real interest. The bedroom closet held a few clothes on wire hangers. The bed had several blankets, but no sheets. On the nightstand was a half-box of .38 special shells, but no weapon. Jack took a mental note since he had never seen Archie with a weapon.

The bathroom was dirty and musty smelling. In the main living room, there was no TV, no stereo, and no family pictures of any kind—nothing that would make it a home.

The second bedroom had some free weights and a small padded weight-lifting bench. But in the closet was something that got Jack's interest: a small safe. Jack got on his knees and turned the dial slowly about a half-turn counter-clockwise. Nothing. Then he turned it in the opposite direction until it clicked. He turned the handle down and pulled, surprised that it opened.

Whoever had opened the safe last had forgotten, or didn't

bother, to spin the dial to clear the combination. Inside was a small cigar box. The folding top had been cut off with a dull knife, leaving it with a torn jagged edge. The box had a wad of money folded in half, with a thick red rubber band holding it tightly closed. It counted out to $1,894. Jack refolded it and placed it back, exactly the same. The box also contained several loose keys. One looked like it was for a safety deposit box. Jack also found a small black address book, with several club members' numbers that he recognized.

The book also contained a dozen other numbers that didn't look familiar. Each was associated with a list of either numbers or letters; some had both running vertically out in the far right column. It was obviously some type of cipher.

Under the address book was a log or daily journal. It also had the same vertical pattern of letters or numbers on the far right column. In the main body of the pages were daily activities for about the last eighteen months. What a stupid practice, Jack thought, to put activities in chronological order. But maybe there was another purpose; one more sinister.

With great reluctance, Jack placed everything back in the safe. He knew that for now at least, he needed to place brotherhood before suspicion. Without any proof, it wasn't right to go meddling in his club brother's private affairs.

Jack spun the knob. That would at least confuse the next person in the safe if they had purposely not spun the knob for quick access to open the safe.

Nothing Jack had run across confirmed his ill feelings about Archie, but nothing acquitted him either. And now Jack liked him even less. He made his way back to the car. All Jack said was "that was a waste." The only question Robert asked was where they were going.

"Cody, Wyoming," was all Jack said.

They met at Pappy's Pancake House in downtown Cody. Jack and Keith sat at a rear booth across from each other. They faced each other for quite a while, not saying much. Jack poured some maple syrup in his coffee and added some cream. His dad always did this for him as a kid—mostly milk, a dollop of syrup, and just a touch of coffee. Keith chained-smoked as he watched Jack prepare the coffee.

Jack broke the silence. "Let me have one of those."

Keith shook the pack until the tan filters popped up. He extended them to Jack.

"I'd prefer one of the Turkish ones," said Jack.

That caused a long pause in the conversation.

Keith looked down, and then back up at Jack. "So you know."

Jack looked grim. "I went back to your room later that night. After you and your friends had left."

Keith lit another cigarette. "They aren't my friends."

"You were all there together."

"Then why are we here talking?"

Jack waited until Keith looked up again. "You owe me an explanation."

"And what do you owe me?"

"A chance to explain?"

Keith balled up his fist. "It was just another mission."

Jack felt as if he'd been punched in the gut. "That's what this has all come down to?" he said. "I'm just another mission?"

Keith couldn't meet Jack's gaze as he told him, "They said you were into some dark shit." He obviously knew his excuse wasn't a good one.

"'They?'" barked Jack. "Who the hell are 'they'? And you believed that? What about you, and me, and what we've been through?"

When Keith didn't respond, Jack continued on, "I made a mistake in Vietnam, I'm not going to do it again here. I'm trying to keep a lid on things. I want that night in that whorehouse to be my last evil deed in this lifetime." Keith paled. "That just happened," he whispered. "It wasn't evil."

Jack's face darkened. "Is that how you're living with it?"

"We said we weren't going to talk about it." Keith clearly didn't want to go there.

"Okay. Let's not. So where does that leave us."

"No harm, no foul?"

"Until next time..."

"Damn it," Keith said to Jack, "there will never be the next time. I was wrong. I knew that on the night in Ventura, and I know that now."

Jack's mind was spinning. "And I should just trust you?"

Keith looked miserable. "That's all I can offer you, Jack. I don't know how else to make this right."

The two men paused and stared at each other. Jack knew he couldn't let Keith walk out of his life, not like this. "Okay, then. I'll accept that."

They both just sat for a moment, and then Keith spoke. "I'm taking some time off to go hunting. Why don't you come with me?"

Jack looked out over the restaurant. "I can't. I've got to get back to Ventura. I'm trying to keep a lid on a major problem."

"Hell, it can wait."

Looking down at his hands, Jack said, "No, it can't. I got some hotheads from back east who want to go to war."

Keith lit another cigarette. "They must have never been in one then."

Jack grimaced. "No, they haven't. And they somehow think it's some kind of noble act."

"Some people need to find out for themselves."

Jack sighed. "Maybe. Not on my watch, though."

Keith looked off into the distance and then back at Jack.

"I think you have some people who want you off the street."

"That's what I am hearing."

Keith looked like he was willing Jack to understand what he

was trying to tell him. "You know those people have their own set of rules."

Jack looked back over at Keith. "I can play that game, too."

"That's dangerous for you."

"It's dangerous for everyone."

"All I'm saying is you need to watch your six."

"Yes, I will. And you watch yours, brother."

With that, Jack said it was time to head home. They shook hands and started to walk away.

"Hey, Jack," Keith called out, "I'm sorry again."

Jack bellowed back, "Semper Fi!"

Keith smiled, his voice breaking as he called back, "Semper Fi!"

Keith felt he had failed Jack again by not telling him about Archie, he went out to his patrol unit and sobbed as Jack disappeared down the street.

Archie was on his way west. He did his best on the flight to rile anyone who would listen. He had a captive audience for several hours, and he took full advantage of every minute. Archie knew the end was around the corner and threw caution to the wind. He was branding Jack not only as a traitor but nothing short of a coward. He found it easy to talk about someone, knowing his accusations would have no day of reckoning.

Silent Bob walked away from Archie's rant. Bob had been around too long to go out like this. He waited until the small group of members in the back of the plane had broken up and then he told Archie, "You know you're swimming in shark-infested waters, my little brother."

Archie immediately went on the defensive. "I know what I see, and I don't like it."

"It seems to me your crowding that man."

Archie wasn't going to back down. "Didya think maybe he was crowding me?"

Silent Bob was taken aback by Archie's attitude. "I'm not sure he's going view it that way."

Archie snarled, "He's not all that special. So what that he was in a war?"

"He don't talk about that," said Silent Bob, clearly surprised that Archie was going to get on that subject, "and I don't think you should either."

"He should keep his nose out of eastern business."

"He sees it as our business," said Silent Bob. "And it really is."

"He should never have met with those assholes."

This was clearly going nowhere fast. "Let's shelf this until we're with him," tried Silent Bob, "and we see what he has to say."

"I'm not interested."

"Hmmm..." said Silent Bob. "It's a mighty thin slice of ham that doesn't have two sides."

The intercom announced they were making their descent into

Los Angeles. The pair took their seats.

The feds had to make a decision. The meeting between the two clubs had thrown their timing off. They knew they had to bring Sherman back into the loop, at least until Bradley could catch up to Archie. A lot would need to be done in a short time once Archie and Gypsy arrived in Indianapolis. Every agent needed to be at the ready when they finally arrived. The feds would cast their net one last time before the end of this operation, pulling whomever they could into it.

When Sherman got the call, he knew it was out of necessity rather than professional protocol. He was positive that the feds had been in and out of town on several occasions without so much as a courtesy call to BET. Sherman's complaints to the chief had fallen on deaf ears. For the chief, it was always about the truckloads of money the feds could drive into his town. He never insisted on a true partnership or thought that it was. His advice to the sergeant was to keep good timesheets and to watch his back.

The chief knew the feds' investigation was winding down. This was all part of grooming Sherman to come up the ranks. He knew the sergeant had some hard lessons to learn if he was going to survive the politics of law enforcement.

Sherman agreed to put agency differences aside, knowing Archie was at risk; he would do his best to protect him. Sherman walked into the coffee room and told Cory to set up a BET meeting.

"What's going on, Boss?"

"We're going to set up surveillance on the Question Marks' clubhouse."

"Starting when?"

"Now."

"I want black-and-white units running by there every fifteen minutes."

"I'll make that call."

"I want them to enter the west end of the street. Have them go east, then turn around at the end of the street and go back west."

"Every fifteen minutes?"

Sherman looked up sharply. "What did I just say?"

"Just checking."

"And have them go nice and slow."

Cory looked perplexed. "What's going on?" he asked. "You want them to see us?"

"Are you listening?"

"I am."

"I want a heavy presence."

Cory finally caught on. "Who we protecting?" he asked.

"No one."

Cory smirked. "So how long will we be protecting no one?"

"Until I say stop."

CHAPTER TWENTY-FOUR

Bikes and cars lined both sides of the street. It was obvious to even a casual observer that something was going on, or at least about to. Jack watched John walk up to the front door of the clubhouse.

"What's with the cops?" John asked.

Jack shrugged. "It started this morning. Every fifteen to twenty minutes."

"Just like this?"

"Yep. Up. Turn around. Then back down. Nice and slow."

John scowled. "Do they talk?"

"Not a word."

John stared at the patrol car. "Goddamn, Jack. You got someone's attention."

"I think it's more than that," replied Jack in a low voice.

"Let's take a walk."

John stopped to light his cigar, and then both men proceeded to the end of the street. They were around the corner before they started their conversation back up.

"The Orphans agreed to open up a line of communication with us," Jack filled in John. "They're willing to try to coexist with us. So I'm sure the meeting I had with the Orphans is connected to the cops—but it's an indirect consequence."

John rubbed his hand down his face. "Jesus Christ! Just say what you mean, Jack."

Jack took a breath.

"Think about it," he told John. "Why would us meeting people halfway across the country bring on all this cop presence?"

John thought a minute. "You're sure it's connected."

Jack nodded. "Yes, we just have to figure out how."

Jack's thoughts turned inward as they walked ahead in silence. Then he spoke aloud. "They're protecting someone."

John stopped. "What are you saying?"

"In the military," Jack explained, "if you want to protect an objective the enemy might want to control, you show a strong presence in hopes of discouraging them from taking action."

"That's certainly one tactic."

Jack went on, his wheels still spinning. "I think that's what's going on. The cops are here to warn us to tread lightly."

"Who are they protecting?" asked John.

Jack looked him in the eye. "You already know what I think."

John didn't respond. They rounded the corner that would take them back to the clubhouse. They headed west as the black-and-white unit passed by eastbound at a crawl.

Bradley was on his way, not that far behind Archie. But far enough that they knew Archie could be in harm's way. The unexpected meeting with the Orphans and then the scheduling of the Ventura meeting had created a logistical nightmare. Bradley was racing to arrive in time to follow Archie and Gypsy on their ride east.

Undercover work was never a precise science; it was always fluid.

The meeting was standing room only. It wasn't just two officers or representatives from each charter who had shown up for it. The general membership had come out in force, too. This was a break in the standard protocol.

Jack rose to address the room. He tried to make eye contact with as many members as possible. The right to left and then back again until he stopped and locked eyes with Archie.

"A lot of things have been said about me lately, things that aren't true." His eyes remained locked with Archie's. "To those people, I say, 'Why tell lies—isn't the truth bad enough?'"

Archie rose and tried to interrupt, but Jack cut him off. "I have the floor."

Jack paused and stared Archie down into submission. Archie acquiesced by taking his seat.

"I'm not a traitor. I'm not a coward. I'm a brother who is concerned about the future of this club. If having concern is wrong, then I'm guilty of that. I took it upon myself to go talk to some men, some men who have a lot in common with us."

Jack ignored the under-the-breath swearing amongst the members and waited for the room to fall back into silence. "You can ask people on both sides, 'Why don't we get along?'" continued Jack. "But no one remembers. It's time to put this behind us. But that's not up to me; it's up to us. I ask you all to tell me: What are we going to do?"

The room broke into a loud rumbling. Old Man John spoke loudly to be heard. "It's an easy thing to do—to keep this problem alive. There are no Orphans out here. But are we men enough to put this behind us? Well, Bob, it's in your backyard. What do you have to say?"

Silent Bob looked around the room. "It's tough. My heart says, 'Fuck the Orphans,' but my head says, 'What's the point anymore?'"

Archie stood up and looked around. "I've kept quiet long enough," he said. "When our two clubs merged, I thought we were on common ground about the Orphans."

"You all joined the Question Marks," Jack shot back. "The clubs didn't merge."

Archie stood with his fists clenched. "I have a right to my opinion."

"We all do," Jack asserted clearly.

"I don't like that club."

Jack shook his head. "You don't have to. But conflicts end at some point. Sometimes, with no real resolution."

John spoke up again and said he was willing to give it a shot if Silent Bob would. And if it didn't work, things could always go back to how they were.

And so it was decided. Jack would hold the responsibility of keeping the line of communication open. The Question Marks would ask for some basic guidelines about territory and conduct when, and if, the two clubs crossed paths in public.

In theory, the Orphans had already agreed to this new protocol. Jimbo had the last word, after all.

Archie knew the police presence was for his safety. At least that's what he was telling himself. He was surrounded by Question Marks. Making a clandestine phone call was out of the question. At least until he and Gypsy got on the road.

But he had to get a message to his backup that he would be leaving soon. He improvised. He pushed his bike out to the front of the clubhouse and positioned it awkwardly. It looked out of place, nosed in with its rear out-of-state plate facing the street, in clear view of the frequent black-and-white units creeping past the rows of bikes.

As the patrol unit crawled by, he could hear the officer calling in his plate numbers. He was counting on the info making it to Sherman in time. Time for what, though, he wasn't sure.

After that, Archie made his presence known, packing and unpacking his saddlebags. Rolling and unrolling his jacket and sleeping bag into compact bundles and placing them on and off the rear of the bike in different positions. He did this several times and hoped for the best.

Archie had tried to fend off Gypsy's bag of pure meth to no avail. When you're standing around talking club politics, the passing around of a bag of crank is like offering a guest a drink at a social function. Stepping out of the ritualistic circle could draw unwanted attention. That was a road Archie could not afford to go down with no backup at the ready.

Archie's mind continued to race, neck-and-neck with his pulse. His tension and paranoia rose higher and higher along with the morning sun. His imagination was starting to run away from him. An inconsequential glance from a member that lasted a moment too long turned into a major debate within his own head.

Whatever direction he turned, someone was watching him, or so he thought. He stood facing the door of the clubhouse. Archie thought he heard his name in an oblique conversation drifting from the open front door of the clubhouse. He knew he was nearing the edge. He convinced himself not to look down; he knew if he did he would see a bottomless pit.

From behind, he heard a voice of solace. It was Sergeant Sherman, parked in the middle of the street, sitting in his black BET unit. He had heard the plate numbers called in over the radio. Sherman called out to Archie, addressing him by the state rocker on his vest. "Hey, Indiana."

Archie turned. "Who me?"

"Didn't I warn you once already?"

Archie was puzzled. Too many thoughts, too much crank.

"About what?"

Sherman barked at him, "If you were going to be in this town for more than ten days to get a California operator's license."

"I've been in and out of town a couple of times."

"And what about this time?"

Archie was relieved. He understood. "I'm planning on leaving for home today."

"So that's with all the gear?"

Archie took a deep breath. "Yeah. I'm heading home."

Sherman continued the rant. "Okay, but if I see you tomorrow, I going to cite you and impound that machine."

"You won't see me."

Archie gathered himself. His message had gotten to Sherman.

He was no longer alone, though still a stranger in a strange land. Was he about to be recognized as a foreigner? Knowing that this would all be coming to an end served as his motivation to keep going. That, and his big plans just over the horizon. Archie had never been a quitter, and his ego was still much bigger than the fear that had been slowly rising within him as each day passed.

Sherman ended his call to Scott. The chief looked across his desk at Sherman. "You looked confused."

"I don't understand why they don't seem to want our help," replied Sherman.

"What you did today was outstanding police work," the chief reassured him. "He called out, and you showed up. If he was in trouble, that was his opportunity to have you arrest him. He could have picked a fight or a dozen other things. What he wanted was for you to pass a message to the feds. You did that."

Sherman stared at the desk. "Scott said Bradley was in town and he would take it from here. I didn't see him." The chief waited until Sherman looked up. "Maybe he didn't want anyone to see him. He's more than capable. It's their operation. BET was never anything more than support."

"Something wasn't right with that agent today," Sherman continued. "He seemed high on something."

"Well, maybe that's why they don't want you too close," the chief agreed. "Don't you have things to do, Sergeant?"

Archie and Gypsy had just pulled out of Vegas. Their fourth gas stop of the day. They ran their engines fast, but not faster than the minds of the two riders piloting them. Gypsy was mentally dividing the pounds of crank into ounces, then the ounces into grams. How would he get his cash home safely?

And maybe the talks with Orphans could be used to his benefit. Gypsy could spread his product throughout the East. And he had heard about the endless supply of weed that the Orphans seemed to have. Weed was becoming big business in California. No more trips to Tijuana for that Mexican dirt weed. It was becoming hard to sell, and the complaints were getting old. Maybe he could make this work in his favor, after all.

Archie grew to like Gypsy, but business was business. Maybe he could turn him, really put a dent in those fucks. Or maybe Gypsy had something on Crest. That was Archie's only regret as this was ending: he wanted to pull that motherfucker Crest into the net. He had let his personal feelings into the mix and had grown to dislike Crest. But at least he wasn't going to have to deal with him any longer. Still, was he confusing fear with aversion? No, he didn't fear him, he assured himself.

Gypsy was setting a hellish pace, and Bradley was having trouble keeping up—even having put tall gears on his drive train for the trip. Archie tried, but couldn't hold Gypsy back. But Bradley was one of the best he had ever worked with; he knew he would find them wherever they stopped for the day.

Archie and Gypsy were somewhere in the desert near the Valley of Fire, with Archie riding to the left of Gypsy. They were doing a slight climb in elevation up into a small pass.

At first, Archie thought a bee had stung him just below his right eye. Within a millisecond, he knew it was no bee. He had been shot. It seemed so fast, yet it all moved slowly.

Archie wasn't sure if he said it out loud or just to himself. But it didn't matter: "Oh my God!" would be his last words on earth.

Everything went black.

Gypsy heard the change in the cadence of the motor and pipes as the throttle of Archie's bike rolled closed. He looked to his left as Archie cascaded off the rear of his bike. Confused, Gypsy backed off his own throttle and watched Archie's bike track straight before veering to the right shoulder.

Gypsy locked his brakes and downshifted to a stop. Then he whipped his bike around and headed back to Archie.

Archie was lying in the number two lane, face up. It seemed so odd; his sunglasses were still in place, held by the tight cord around his head, but they were crooked on his face.

Gypsy had never seen a gunshot victim. He tried to keep his composure but was losing ground. Trucks were stopped on the road and backing up. Some were parking along the shoulder.

"What the fuck happened?" called out a trucker.

Gypsy didn't answer. His ears were ringing from the day's ride, and his mind was racing from what had just happened. The same trucker ran over. "I'll be goddamned—this boy's been shot. He's deader than hell."

The shooter made sure there would be no easy access off the stretch of road he had chosen. No turn-offs until the other side of the crest. He would be long gone before any type of coordinated investigation could get underway.

Shooting at a down angle had served him well. He was confident it had been a kill shot. If not, there was still Archie's fall off the bike.

Keith made his way back to his vehicle for a leisurely trip home, stopping to hunt and fish. All his SWAT gear was in plain sight, on the chance he encountered any nosy lawmen. He was just another cop coming home from a training exercise.

Keith felt that he and Jack were once again square. The playing field was now even.

Keith had arrived in Ventura the night before the scheduled meeting at the clubhouse. He had found himself a well-hidden vantage point on the hill overlooking the whole scene. By chance, it was not far from the spot where Bradley had watched several months earlier on the night of the grenade attack.

Archie hadn't been hard to spot; he was continually packing and unpacking his bike.

Keith had heard the black-and-white unit call the plate numbers on his portable scanner. And he'd watched with contempt Sherman and Archie's theatrical performance on the street below.

Keith had actually considered taking the shot from the hill above the clubhouse then and there, but it was too risky. Besides, he had left the rifle in his vehicle. He decided to stick to his original plan and wait for one of the three positions he had chosen on the way out of town.

His plan worked.

CHAPTER TWENTY-FIVE

Bradley pulled up as the accident investigation site was transitioning into a homicide crime scene. He pulled his van in between the flares. The Nevada Highway Patrol had taken control.

"What the hell do you think you're doing?" one officer immediately called out to Bradley.

Bradley looked at him. "Why don't you tell me what's going on here, trooper."

It was a rhetorical request used to take command of the situation. Bradley could see exactly what was going on as he surveyed the scene. Archie was still lying on the highway; he hadn't even been covered yet. Gypsy's right wrist was handcuffed to the door of NHP unit. Bradley flipped his government identification. "Why is he cuffed?"

"A safety issue, sir."

"Cut him loose."

Bradley called out to Gypsy by name. "Stand over there. You and I need to talk."

Gypsy stared at Bradley, trying to place this man who seemed to know him. But no such luck; he was drawing a blank.

Sergeant Jones was back in his Las Vegas Metro office. He had gotten the call with the details of the murder that had happened just east of his town. His first call was to Sergeant Sherman.

"Remember me? Jones, Vegas Metro?"

"I do, Sergeant," replied Sherman without hesitation.

Jones got straight to the point. "Got a couple of your motorcycle boys east of here. One of them shot dead."

"Who would that be?"

"An Archie Skinner out of Indiana."

"Damn!" Sherman sat up in his chair. "Are you sure? He's a good guy."

"No shit? Maybe you need to be out here."

Sherman figured he'd let Jones in on what was happening. "Skinner's a fed ... but they cut me loose."

"Then I would come out here right away and cover my ass if I were you."

Bradley had the state troopers get word to Washington. Ingram would take control of the more sensitive aspects of the situation.

Any investigation into Archie's death would net them nothing. Bradley knew this within a few minutes of his arrival. It was clear that somebody who had professional training and experience was responsible for this. But Bradley went through the motions to cover his ass.

It was going to be a volatile ride for the next few days.

The pending internal investigation could be even worse. He let the NHP call the investigation. Archie Skinner headed back to Vegas in a body bag, and Gypsy went cuffed in the back of a patrol unit. In Ventura, Sherman persuaded the chief to let him appropriate the county patrol plane for the trip to Nevada. It cruised at a cool 125 mph, and Sherman was in Vegas in under three hours. Sergeant Jones was waiting when he arrived.

The first thing, after a brief catch-up conversation with Jones, was a request from Sherman: "I need to see the toxicology report on the dead agent."

"I can make that happen," replied Jones.

Sherman followed Jones into the County Coroner's office and noticed Bradley standing in the hall. As always, Bradley was all business.

"We got us a real mess, Sergeant," he told him. "There is nothing else we can do here. They told us the shot severed his brain stem, and in all likelihood, he was dead before he left the bike. It's good to have you guys here. We have a short window of time."

"For what?" Sherman quizzed him.

"To turn Gypsy," Bradley responded quickly. "It's going to take the three of us."

He turned to Sherman's companion. "So I'll have to trust you, Jones."

Jones couldn't hide his surprise. "How do you know my name?"

"Your name tag." Bradley pointed. They all had a chuckle as Bradley repeated. "I can do that, yes?"

"Do what?"

"Trust you."

Everyone shook hands.

Keith was leaving Arizona and coming into Utah. He was just west of St. George when he neared the scales that greeted all trucks crossing the state line. He could see the long line of red taillights of backed up traffic. A row of red flares glowed across the highway rerouting all of the vehicles into the weigh station. He lit a cigarette and waited his turn.

The young officer asked where he had been and where he was headed. Purposely, Keith flipped open his wallet exposing both his police and military identification. After a quick look, the officer waved off the wallet.

Keith closed it. "I was in L.A. doing a little SWAT training. They're the best in the country."

"So I hear."

The officer shone his light on the SWAT gear and then shifted the bright beam to the rifle case and fishing gear.

Keith looked at the lighted equipment. "Took a working vacation. Stopped and did a little hunting, too. Now I'm going up 89 to do some fishing."

"Boy, I envy you. Any luck hunting?"

Keith smiled at the irony. "Nothing I can talk about." They both laughed, and he drove on.

Bradley and both sergeants walked into the interrogation room.

"I said to keep those cuffs off of him," Bradley told Jones.

As he unlocked Gypsy's cuffs, Jones casually replied, "It was only procedure."

Deep red rings encircled each of Gypsy's wrists. Bradley offered him a smoke, lighting Gypsy's first, then his own.

"Have you called home?"

"No, I haven't called anywhere."

"I think you should call."

"So do I."

Bradley walked him out to the phone and then stepped away.

Gypsy picked up the receiver.

In the next room, the reel-to-reel started turning, recording every word. Bradley placed the headphones up to his ears. He listened to the line ring three times, and then Robert answered.

Bradley could hear the tension in Gypsy's voice. "Hey, I need to talk to Jack."

"He's not here," replied Robert. "Haven't seen him."

Robert could be heard calling out to the room, but no one had any idea where Jack had gone.

Gypsy told Robert what had happened out on the road. But it

was difficult to understand what Gypsy was even talking about. The details were unclear even to Gypsy, and he was there when it happened.

"He's dead," Gypsy just kept repeating. "They shot Archie off his bike."

Robert seemed to have trouble coming up with how to respond. His eventual reply was simple: "Jesus! I'll call Silent Bob and try to find Jack."

Bradley got two major pieces of information from that little conversation: No one had seen Crest, so he was now a suspect in Bradley's book, and Gypsy had failed to mention that the police had him. He never mentioned that he was at the Vegas Metro Station or that he had just been sitting with Bradley and his men.

Now that was promising.

Sherman led Gypsy back into the interrogation room where Bradley returned and began talking to Gypsy.

"I'm going to tell you what I know," Bradley said, "then I'm going to tell you what I think. I want you to just listen. Don't interrupt me. Do you understand?"

Gypsy didn't open his mouth; he just nodded.

Bradley addressed him by his first name. The name no one dared to call him to his face. "That's a good start, Clarence. I like that you know how to listen. Now, listen. Several months before the Saints From Hell became Question Marks, we placed a plant in with them. Mind you, not an informant, an actual ATF Agent. You and all your buddies knew him as Archie Skinner. And as you know, somebody shot and killed him today. So, as of right now, you are either a witness or an accomplice to murder. It's not looking so good for you, any way you cut it."

Gypsy paled, and Bradley continued on, "You are engaged in a drug conspiracy with Agent Skinner, as well as other Question Mark members. You have also committed overt acts. Let me explain to you what an 'overt act' is. You personally have sent materials, to manufacture meth at an address that I supplied to you through our murdered agent. Not to mention that I know all about the P2P that you ordered and paid for in advance. Oh, and did I mention that all the conversations were taped?"

Gypsy looked like he was going to lose it any minute, so Bradley decided to move on quickly. "Some of my colleagues believe that you discovered that Archie was, in fact, an ATF Agent. You told Crest, and then you conspired with Crest to eliminate our agent.

"It's common knowledge that Crest hated Archie. In fact, we also have that on tape. Jack Crest has not been around. No one has seen him. That would have given him the time to drive out here. We all know about Crest's past and what he's capable of. You can't deny any of it, and that makes him a suspect.

"So with all that," Bradley summed up, "it's an understatement to say that you're in way over your head."

Bradley looked over at Sergeant Jones. "How do they treat cop killers in this state?"

Both sergeants stared right through Gypsy and said nothing.

Bradley turned back to Gypsy. "But the good news is that I am going to offer you a way out. You cooperate with me and my associates, all of your troubles disappear. We wire you up, you get Crest on tape talking about the murder of Archie. I guarantee you a cash payout, and then you can disappear."

Bradley offered Gypsy another cigarette. "Relax; enjoy your smoke. You can give me your answer when you finish it."

While they waited, Bradley mused to no one in particular. "That was a hell of a shot today. I'm not sure I could have made it. They'll be talking about that one for quite a while."

Jones joined in the macabre conversation. "Our SWAT team's got some excellent snipers."

"Do you think Crest is that good?" asked Sherman.

No one answered, and they all sat in silence, watching and waiting for the smoke and the time ran out.

As Gypsy tamped his smoke out, Bradley spoke up. "So, what's it going to be?"

"I'm on board," said Gypsy in a low voice. "What do I need to do?"

Bradley smiled like a Cheshire cat. "Sergeant Jones will have your bike released to you. Go back to the Ventura clubhouse and then go home. I will contact you once things settle down a bit.

"For now, I expect you to act pissed off. Someone has killed your club brother, Archie. Once the story breaks that he was an undercover ATF Agent, you see if you can get Crest to talk about the murder."

Bradley thought for a moment. "Before you go, you need to call them again. See if they have located Crest. Tell them you're coming home."

The two men stared at each other until it became uncomfortable. Clarence looked away.

Jack had waited at the clubhouse for Archie and Gypsy to depart. There was no way he was going to leave his two main adversaries alone with a large audience. As soon as Jack was gone, they would have rabble-roused anyone who would listen to join in their assault on his character. His position as a leader was strong at the moment, but politics in any society is subject to immediate change. Jack had come too far too fast to let that happen.

He watched as they pulled away from the curb to start their journey east. He hadn't gotten much sleep since the meeting with the Orphans, and he knew that it was starting to take its toll on him. He had purposely parked his truck around the corner. Without a goodbye to anyone, he slipped away and made his way to Nikki's. He joined her for breakfast and then climbed into her bed where he spent the next twenty-four hours.

Nikki spent an uneventful day at work and returned home that evening to join Jack in bed. In the morning, they would each return to their separate worlds, worlds that were about to collide.

Gypsy made calls not only to Ventura but to other charters that he thought would be influential in supporting the lie of Jack's participation in the murder of club brother Archie Skinner. Vegas Metro, at the request of Bradley, trucked Gypsy and his bike just west of Victorville. Gypsy arrived in Ventura in a little over five hours and stood in front of a very active clubhouse.

Gypsy told his story over and over to anyone who would listen.

But he was very careful not to step across the line of accusations. He didn't have to; there was already talk of kicking Jack out of the club. The negative perception spread across the club like a tsunami making its way inland from a shoreline.

Nikki arrived at work and was called straight into her editor. She was caught off guard by his brusque manner. "When was the last time you saw Crest?"

She answered her own question: "Why?"

He turned to look out the window. "Find him. One of his gang got shot off his bike last night, and I want a statement."

Nikki didn't hesitate. "Where?"

"Outside of Vegas."

He waved her away as a dismissal. "Now get that statement!" he barked.

Nikki called her house and used the signal for Jack to pick up the phone. One ring, hang up and then call back. No answer. The clubhouse rang busy, which was to be expected if it were true a member had been murdered.

Jack pulled up to a clubhouse in chaos. The old man standing out on the street was a clear signal that something serious had happened. He was puffing so hard on his cigar, he resembled a factory smokestack.

Jack got out of his truck as John approached him, and Robert seemed to appear from nowhere. Robert looked at Jack and then lifted his shirt up ever-so-slightly to reveal the butt of a semi-auto pistol that was stuffed in his pants.

"You got a tiger by the tail here."

Jack knew he was missing something important. "What are you talking about?"

John stared into his eyes. "Archie's been shot dead. Out in the desert. A long-distance shot. Blown right off his bike."

John moved over to the hood of Jack's truck.

Jack stared right back at John, never blinking. "John, I've been asleep since I left here yesterday. Is it cold enough to pass your miles test?"

John appeared embarrassed by the amateur attempt at detective work.

"I don't know anything about what happened," continued Jack. "And I'm sorry that a Question Mark has been killed. But this doesn't change a thing about how I feel about him—I mean how I felt about him. I never liked him, and I'm not going to pretend that I ever felt anything different."

"There are people in that clubhouse ready to kick you out of the club," the old man somberly told him.

Jack looked at John and Robert. "Well then, let's go see what they have to say to my face."

The reception was cold as Jack entered the main room. Conversations either hushed or ended abruptly. Jack looked around the room. "Does somebody have something they want to say?"

The moment hung in the air. All eyes averted from Jack's glare.

"It's no secret that I didn't like Archie," Jack told the room, "but that's not a good enough reason for me to kill a brother."

Jack walked to the stove and poured himself a cup of coffee. He then situated himself, so his back was to the farthest corner. With Robert at his right shoulder, he surveyed the room slowly and carefully.

When Nikki watched the press conference on the network news, the first lie that stood-out was that the man who had introduced himself to her as Robert Maxwell several weeks earlier was now standing at the podium identifying himself as Bob Ingram, and he was with several other men from various agencies. She was positive it was him, right down to the Annapolis class ring. Each bureaucrat stepped forward to get his moment of fame.

After the introductions, Ingram began his statement: "It is with great regret and a heavy heart that I make this announcement today: Yesterday, east of Las Vegas, Nevada, law enforcement lost a brave young man. He had been working in an undercover capacity for over twenty-four months at great risk to himself. He put his personal safety aside to make sure this great country will continue to be one of the safest societies on this planet..."

The political rhetoric continued. Ingram explained the basis of the operation, and how one of their men had been killed by a sniper. He went on to explain that not only would the operation continue forward, but that an arrest was imminent in the murder of ATF Agent Lester Combs, who had used the name Archie Skinner in his undercover capacity. No questions were taken at the conference since the investigation was "in progress."

It was about 3:30 p.m. on the West Coast when the conference concluded. It wasn't long before Nikki's desk phone rang. It was

Robert Maxwell asking her if she was interested in the story they had discussed.

Nikki said that she was, but told him that before they got started, they had some things that needed to be straightened out.

The early satellite feed beaming into the dish atop her newspaper's building had allowed its staff to get the six o'clock news three hours earlier than the rest of the West Coast.

Nikki informed "Maxwell" about the luxury the satellite feed afforded her office, giving it an edge in many areas. She then informed him how important it was for her to know with whom she was speaking. Ingram stopped her and apologized for using an alias.

"It was a precaution that I had to take because our main target was local resident Jack Crest."

"Why was the ATF involved in a drug case and not the DEA?" Nikki quickly questioned Ingram.

"This started as a weapons case," he told her, "but it made a transition into narcotics. The case developed a life of its own. Both agencies are relatively new, and it's just the way we continued the investigation. Jack Crest is now the main suspect in the murder of Agent Combs. It's only a matter of time before we make an arrest."

Nikki began to feel uncomfortable, knowing she could end this allegation with a simple admission that Jack had been asleep in her bed. As Ingram repeated his previous accusations, Nikki interrupted. "Are you saying Crest killed what he thought to be one of his own guys? That doesn't make sense."

"I know you're familiar with BET," Ingram responded. "I've read the previous articles you wrote. BET had knowledge that Question Mark member Archie Skinner was an undercover ATF Agent."

Nikki knew she needed to pin him down. "Is that on the record?"

"I would prefer to remain an unnamed source, but would go on the record if challenged."

"Are you also saying that they were the leak?"

Ingram skirted the direct answer. "It sure the hell wasn't us. You can draw your own conclusions."

It was around five o'clock West Coast time when Silent Bob called the Ventura clubhouse. He had seen, along with many other members, the press conference about the murder of the undercover ATF agent. The political tsunami that had almost swept over Jack receded. With the press conference exposing Archie Skinner as a traitor to the Question Marks, Jack's denials now fell on even deafer ears. The members believed what they wanted, and most took the position that Jack's actions—whether he admitted to them or not—had steered the club away from an impending storm to safety.

Within hours of the press conference, Jack's political might within the Question Mark empire became unchallenged. He spent the rest of the evening holding court with anyone who could get an audience with him.

Among those showing their respect was Gypsy, who made every effort to get Jack to talk about Archie.

Nikki had three people she needed to talk to Jack, her editor, and Sherman. She headed to BET headquarters first and entered unannounced.

She found Sherman to be both professional and committed to destroying Jack Crest. He gave her a complete tour of BET headquarters, including what he coined as the wall of shame. It was very similar to the structure of traditional organized crime. It consisted of a tree of names, pictures, and comments. And of course, Jack was at the top. After the tour, they sat in Sherman's office discussing the investigation in general and then moved on to the murder.

Nikki looked directly at Sherman. "What would you say if I told you the feds are claiming that the leak of the agent's undercover status that led to his murder came from BET?" Sherman looks offended. "I would say that's impossible."

Nikki tilted her head. "Impossible or unlikely?"

Sherman spoke slowly. "Impossible. I am the only one who knew."

Nikki pondered. "Why would they say that?"

Sherman shrugged. "Well, someone's got to answer for that murder. The feds are trying to deflect it from themselves—whether they blame BET or the Question Marks. You know, Crest is really the only winner in this entire mess."

Nikki wasn't sure where Sherman was headed. "Why is that?"

"Everyone thinks Crest did it," he explained. "In my opinion, no one will ever prove it. To his club, he'll now be a hero. He took out the cop who was trying to destroy his men."

"You think he did it?"

Sherman had already thought this through. “I think he had the motive. Certainly, the talent. The opportunity, I don’t know. That remains to be seen.”

Sherman decided he needed someone on BET’s side. “What if I told you that murdered agent was using drugs?”

Nikki’s eyebrows raised. “I would say, ‘Prove it.’“

Sherman gave a satisfied smile. “I have a preliminary autopsy report. It shows levels of meth and traces of barbiturates.”

He handed her the report that Sergeant Jones had faxed him.

Nikki looked over the report. “What’s that have to do with the murder?”

Sherman shook his head. “He went outside the guidelines. Maybe he made a mistake. Either way, if you’re going to write this story, that should be a part of it. Do you think you can write a nonbiased story?”

“Why would you ask me that?” asked Nikki, irritated.

Sherman gave nothing away. “I just had to ask you, that’s all.”

Nikki thanked him and exited his office. She dropped a quarter into the payphone outside and listened to the series of rings.

“Jack Crest, please.”

A gruff voice said, “Hang on...”

She could hear a lot of background noise coming through the handset.

“It sounds like a party’s going on,” she said when Jack came on the line.

"Yeah."

Nikki voiced her question, "Victory party?"

"I'm not in the habit of celebrating death," replied Jack.

"Not even for special occasions?" pushed Nikki.

"Well, maybe."

Nikki turned serious. "I need to see you."

"It's really hectic here."

Nikki knew exactly what to say. "Even for me, Jack?"

"I can't leave," Jack explained.

"Can't or won't?" Nikki had to see him.

Jack finally sensed something was wrong. "Can you come here?"

"I need to talk to you alone."

"We can take a walk," Jack assured her.

Satisfied, Nikki replied, "Give me thirty minutes."

At headquarters Bradley was with Ingram and Scott, trying to reconstruct their investigation. They had taken a big hit. They were long past discussing what went wrong and now had to focus on how to fix it. Bradley brought them up to speed on their new operative. There was much to do in a short amount of time if they were going to succeed in getting things back on track. Bradley would travel to the West Coast alone, which was always his preference. He had a lot of work to do with Gypsy.

Jack moved to the front of the clubhouse and waited for Nikki to arrive. For the last several hours, Robert had shadowed his every move.

"I need to talk to Nikki alone," Jack told him.

Robert didn't say a word; he just nodded.

As Nikki approached the clubhouse, she could see that there had already been a major shift in Jack's status with his brothers.

The two always kept their greetings reserved in public.

Jack suggested they take a walk. They traveled the same route around the block that Old Man John and Jack had traveled only days earlier. This path would be repeated over and over in years to come to avoid any real or suspected surveillance.

After turning the corner, Nikki said, "I've had some interesting conversations as of late."

Jack glanced at Nikki. "I'm sure you have."

Nikki sighed. "I'm working on a story, and I think you should know."

"So this is a professional visit?" Jack asked tersely.

"Well, both personal and professional," replied Nikki quickly.

"Isn't that dangerous in your business?"

"Maybe in yours; not mine," Nikki shot back.

Jack stopped and turned towards Nikki. "I didn't kill that agent. I may have never liked him, but that was no secret. That's my statement."

Nikki looked over Jack's shoulder. "Or do you mean your story?"

Jack softly gripped her chin. "Nikki, don't start."

She looked up at him. "What about all the other allegations?"

His tone brooked no argument. "I don't engage in illegal activities."

Nikki took hold of his wrist. "What about your associates?"

He never let go. "I can't speak for them. As a club, my position is no, we don't."

Nikki's voice was flat. "That's it? It's that cut and dry? That easy?"

Jack's tone was just as flat. "You're writing a story. Well, that's my input."

Nikki had to put it all out there. "And you're standing in the club?"

He sucked in a breath. "You know my position. I'm one of the leaders."

Nikki knew she was difficult, maybe because she hated having to do this. "I was told you are now the leader."

Jack shrugged. "Maybe in a de facto sense."

Her mouth pressed into a hard line. "So, it's Hail, Caesar?"

Jack didn't want to fight. "Stop it. Don't be an asshole. Why are you writing this story? Never mind. I know why. It's because that's what you do and you're good at it. I'd never take that away from you. But this is what I do. Please don't take that away from me."

Nikki could feel a tear rolling from her eye. “Damn you, Jack Crest.”

Jack released her chin and used his thumb to wipe the tear away.

She grabbed his hand. “Let’s not become the people who are chasing you.”

Jack pressed his forehead to hers. “Is that a dare?”

Nikki smiled. “Yes, it is.”

Nikki stood at her desk putting her notes in order for her meeting with her editor. She wasn’t about to be late. Like most old-school editors, every aspect of his life was on a deadline.

She walked into his office and dropped her notes on his desk. “I think I am going to recuse myself from this story.”

Her editor looked over his glasses, picked up his cold cup of coffee, and raised it to his lips. As he was returning his cup to the desk, Nikki saw realization draw on his features.

“Jesus Christ, Nikki. You’re fucking Crest!”

Nikki didn’t reply.

He tossed the bundle back in her direction. “It’s your story, and you’re going to write it. I want Crest in it, and I want him named as a suspect in that agent’s murder.”

Nikki stood her ground. “I don’t feel strongly about that theory.”

Her editor compromised. “Okay, a person of interest then. Get it done; that’s our lead story tomorrow.”

Robert walked over to Jack to let him know Gypsy was on the

phone.

"Yeah."

Gypsy got right to the point. "It's Gypsy. I'd like to come up and talk with you."

"I think that's a good idea," replied Jack.

"How about tomorrow?"

"Sunday is Robert's birthday," Jack told him. "How about then?"

"Sounds good."

"We can have dinner at the pier, on me."

Gypsy seemed surprised by the offer. "Thanks, Jack. Perfect. See you then."

It proved to be an awkward meal.

Anyone who ventures into the underworld learns very quickly that the way to longevity is to not ask a lot of questions.

Gypsy was breaking outlaw protocol by asking Jack if he was involved in the death of Archie. And when he didn't get the answer he wanted, he would restructure the question and ask it again.

When Gypsy got no satisfaction from Jack, he moved on to Robert in his pursuit of answers.

He was asking a lot of questions.

Gypsy returned home one night to find his answer staring him in the face. When he turned on the light, there was Jack sitting in the wooden rocking chair by the fireplace. But it wasn't positioned toward the red brick opening any longer; it now faced the front door. Jack gestured for him to move deeper into the room.

Gypsy could see that Jack was holding a long-barreled black .22 LR semi-automatic pistol. It was equipped with a long, slender black silencer. Next to the rocker was a round lamp table. On the table was an ashtray full of half-smoked butts from Bradley's Turkish cigarettes.

Not taking his eyes off Gypsy, Jack motioned the table with a slight jerk of his head to indicate the butt-filled dish.

Jack now had a question of his own: "Anything you'd like me to tell Bradley when I catch up to him?"

For a brief moment, Gypsy started to unravel but then composed himself. He knew how this would end. "Yeah, tell him to go to hell. And you can, too."

"That-a-boy, Gypsy."

With that remark, Jack shot him twice in the center of his chest. Gypsy dropped to his knees, and his arms remained at his sides. His chin rested on his chest as if he was trying to inspect his wounds as he fell forward. The wooden floor let out a thump as his face, and the wood collided. Gypsy's arms never left his side.

The rocker swayed gently from the two gunshots, as Jack slowly rose. The blood was pooling on both sides of Gypsy's chest. Jack passed by him lying face down on the floor and put one last shot in the back of his head.

Blood pumped out, but more slowly now. He was dead or dying. Jack glanced over his shoulder and told all the lost souls who had been following him to stay with Gypsy. He didn't look back but was sure they were no longer behind him. Jack had sealed his destiny.

He got into the car and asked Robert to take the coast highway back to Ventura.

EPILOGUE

Nikki's story made national news. No one was spared, all the way down to law enforcement's interest in Jack as a participant in two murders. It was an indictment to everyone involved. The murder of an undercover agent—as well as club member Gypsy's cooperation with the government and his subsequent death—launched an Attorney General's Office internal inquest.

The eventual conclusion was that the use of narcotics diminished Archie's judgment and had compromised him. The ATF's position was that he was forced to use the drugs to keep his undercover identity secure. The agent's integrity never came into question publicly, but in private he became the scapegoat for anyone who came under scrutiny during the inquest.

ATF Agent Scott received a promotion of sorts, but no longer worked as a field agent.

After an Internal Affairs investigation in Ventura County, Sergeant Sherman was cleared of any wrongdoing. There was no credible evidence that he had compromised the security of the undercover ATF agent. To appease the feds, and on paper, the BET unit was disbanded. In principle, it remained intact and in the same location.

It was now known as SIU, Special Investigation Unit, still headed by a newly promoted Lieutenant Sherman. This ensured that the federal money would continue to roll in.

Bob Ingram and Bill Bradley managed to elude the heart of the inquiry. They continued to work as a team and were placed on the ground floor of a new political movement in Nicaragua. They began aiding a group of freedom fighters that would come to be known as the Contras.

Ingram's obscurity ended when he was called to testify before the Iran-Contra hearings. Bradley always seemed to be one step ahead of things and disappeared into Afghanistan. While there, he worked with Afghan Anti-Soviet forces.

Nikki and Jack's relationship continued but was strained. Nikki came to terms with her own ethics and told her boss this would be her last story on the Question Marks or Jack Crest.

The attack on the clubhouse remained unsolved. Jack was certain it had been Bill Bradley acting alone, and he patiently waited for the day they would meet again.

Both federal and local law enforcement agencies held Jack responsible for the murder of both Archie Skinner—Lester Combs—and Gypsy; if not by his hand personally, at the very least, by his order. This started a vendetta that appeared to have no end. The following year at Sturgis, both the Question Marks and the Orphans flooded the streets shoulder to shoulder and had no problems. Both clubs finally acknowledged that Jack was right: they had more in common than they had realized.

Coming back from Sturgis, Jack stopped in Cody to visit with

Keith.

This would become an annual tradition on his return trip home, but neither would ever again discuss his private or professional life. They were just two veterans who celebrated their return home from a war with a few days of fishing each year.

They never mentioned the events of the last few months, the dead ATF agent, or about the empty shell-casing Keith pushed across the table to Jack.

Nothing needed to be said.

Jack arrived at the fishing hole as the sun was starting its daily ascent. He studied the shoreline carefully and bit into one of the fried egg sandwiches he had made the night before. He had to admit it wasn't as good as the ones his dad used to make, but it was damn close.

After careful consideration, Jack picked his spot to cast.

The monofilament line sang as the hooks and weights pulled it into the surf. He let the line settle on the ocean bottom then set the break on his peen reel. He adjusted the drag and began his wait. He watched and waited, carefully studying the end of his pole. He was trying to distinguish between the bounces. Were they fish strikes or the current pulling on the weights at the end of the line?

Jack still used the same gear his parents had put under the Christmas tree so many years before. As that thought crossed his mind, for a brief moment, Jack thought he could hear his parents laughing. He looked up the beach expecting to see them, but it was just the wind carrying the cry of the seagulls to him.

END